Deadfalls and Snares

A. R. Harding

Deadfalls and Snares

The present edition is a reproduction of previous publication of this classic work. Minor typographical errors may have been corrected without note; however, for an authentic reading experience the spelling, punctuation, and capitalization have been retained from the original text.

ISBN: 978-1-63637-802-2

CONTENTS

	Introduction	iv
I	Building Deadfalls	1
II	Bear and Coon Deadfall	11
III	Otter Deadfall	14
IV	Marten Deadfall	17
V	Stone Deadfall	23
VI	The Bear Pen	31
VII	Portable Traps	36
VIII	Some Triggers	42
IX	Trip Triggers	46
X	How to Set	51
XI	When to Build	55
XII	Where to Build	57
XIII	The Proper Bait	61
XIV	Traps Knocked Off	63
XV	Spring Pole Snare	65
XVI	Trail Set Snare	71
XVII	Bait Set Snare	76
XVIII	The Box Trap	81
XIX	The Coop Trap	84
XX	The Pit Trap	86
XXI	Number of Traps	88
XXII	When to Trap	90
XXIII	Season's Catch	93
XXIV	General Information	96
XXV	Skinning and Stretching	100
XXVI	Handling and Grading	116
XXVII	From Animal to Market	122
XXVIII	Steel Traps	127

INTRODUCTION

Scattered from the Arctic Ocean to the Gulf of Mexico and from the Atlantic to the Pacific Ocean are thousands of trappers who use deadfalls, snares and other home-made traps, but within this vast territory there are many thousand who know little or nothing of them.

The best and most successful trappers are those of extended experience. Building deadfalls and constructing snares, as told on the following pages, will be of value to trappers located where material — saplings, poles, boards, rocks, etc. — is to be had for constructing. The many traps described cannot all be used to advantage in any section, but some of them can.

More than sixty illustrations are used to enable the beginner to better understand the constructing and workings of home-made traps. The illustrations are mainly furnished by the "old timers."

Chapters on Skinning and Stretching, Handling and Grading are added for the correct handling of skins and furs adds largely to their commercial value.

A. R. Harding

CHAPTER I

BUILDING DEADFALLS

During the centuries that trapping has been carried on, not only in America, but thruout the entire world, various kinds of traps and snares have been in use and taken by all classes of trappers and in all sections the home-made traps are of great numbers. The number of furs caught each year is large.

The above was said by a trapper some years ago who has spent upwards of forty years in the forests and is well acquainted with traps, trappers and fur-bearing animals. Whether the statement is true or not, matters but little, altho one thing is certain and that is that many of the men who have spent years in trapping and have been successful use the deadfalls and snares as well as steel traps.

Another trapper says: In my opinion trapping is an art and any trapper that is not able to make and set a deadfall, when occasion demands, does not belong to the profession. I will give a few of the many reasons why dead falls are good.

1. There is no weight to carry.

2. Many of the best trappers use them.

3. It requires no capital to set a line of deadfalls.

4. There is no loss of traps by trap thieves, but the fur is in as much danger.

5. Deadfalls do not mangle animals or injure their fur.

6. It is a humane way of killing animals.

7. There is no loss by animals twisting off a foot or leg and getting away.

8. Animals are killed outright, having no chance to warn others of their kind by their cries from being caught.

9. Trappers always have the necessary outfit (axe and knife) with them to make and set a deadfall that will kill the largest animals.

10. The largest deadfalls can be made to spring easy and catch small game if required.

1

11. Deadfalls will kill skunk without leaving any scent.

12. Deadfalls are cheap and trappers should be familiar with them.

It is a safe proposition, however, that not one-half of the trappers of today can build a deadfall properly or know how to make snares, and many of them have not so much as seen one.

First a little pen about a foot square is built of stones, chunks, or by driving stakes close together, leaving one side open. The stakes should be cut about thirty inches long and driven into the ground some fourteen inches, leaving sixteen or thereabout above the ground. Of course if the earth is very solid, stakes need not be so long, but should be so driven that only about sixteen inches remain above ground. A sapling say four inches in diameter and four feet long is laid across the end that is open. A sapling that is four, five or six inches in diameter, owing to what you are trapping for, and about twelve feet long, is now cut for the "fall." Stakes are set so that this pole or fall will play over the short pole on the ground. These stakes should be driven in pairs; two about eighteen inches from the end; two about fourteen farther back. (See illustration.)

THE POLE DEADFALL

The small end of the pole should be split and a small but stout stake driven firmly thru it so there will be no danger of the pole turning and "going off" of its own accord. The trap is set by placing the prop (which is only seven inches in length and half an inch thru) between the top log and the short one on the ground, to which is attached the long trigger, which is only a stick about the size of the prop, but about twice as long, the baited end of which extends back into the little pen.

The bait may consist of a piece of chicken, rabbit or any tough bit of meat so long as it is fresh and the bloodier the better. An animal on scenting the bait will reach into the trap — the top of the pen having been carefully covered over — between the logs. When the animal seizes the bait the long trigger is pulled off of the upright prop and down comes the fall, killing the animal by its weight. Skunk, coon, opossum, mink and in fact nearly all kinds of animals are easily caught in this trap. The fox is an exception, as it is rather hard to catch them in deadfalls.

The more care that you take to build the pen tight and strong, the less liable is some animal to tear it down and get bait from the outside; also if you will cover the pen with leaves, grass, sticks, etc., animals will not be so shy of the trap. The triggers are very simple, the long one being placed on top of the upright, or short one. The long triggers should have a short prong left or a nail driven in it to prevent the game from getting the bait off too easy. If you find it hard to get saplings the right size for a fall, and are too light, they can be weighted with a pole laid on the "fall."

I will try and give directions and drawing of deadfalls which I have used to some extent for years, writes a Maine trapper, and can say that most all animals can be captured in them as shown in illustration. You will see the deadfall is constructed of stakes and rocks and is made as follows: Select a place where there is game; you need an axe, some nails, also strong string, a pole four inches or more in diameter. Notice the cut No. 1 being the drop pole which should be about six to seven feet long. No. 2 is the trip stick, No. 3 is string tied to pole and trip stick, No. 4 is the stakes for holding up the weight, No. 5 is the small stakes driven around in the shape of letter U, should be one foot wide and two feet long. No. 6 is the rocks, No. 7 is the bait.

3

SMALL ANIMAL FALL

Now this is a great trap for taking skunk and is soon built where there are small saplings and rocks. This trap is also used for mink and coon.

The trapper's success depends entirely upon his skill and no one can expect the best returns unless his work is skillfully done. Do not Attempt to make that deadfall unless you are certain that you can make it right and do not leave it till you are certain that it could not be any better made. I have seen deadfalls so poorly made and improperly set that they would make angels weep, neither were they located where game was apt to travel. The deadfall if made right and located where game frequents is quite successful.

Another thing, boys, think out every little plan before you attempt it. If so and so sets his traps one way, see if you can't improve on his plan and make it a little better. Do not rush blindly into any new scheme, But look at it on all sides and make yourself well acquainted with the merits and drawbacks of it. Make good use of your brains, for the animal instinct is its only protection and it is only by making good use of your reasoning powers that you can fool him. Experience may cost money sometimes and loss of patience and temper, but in my estimation it is the trapper's best capital. An old trapper who has a couple of traps and lots of experience will catch more fur than the greenhorn with a complete outfit. Knowledge is power in trapping as in all other trades.

This is the old reliable "pinch-head." The picture does not show the cover, so I will describe it. Get some short pieces of board or short poles and lay them on the stones in the back part of the pen and on the raised stick in front. Lay them close together so the animal cannot crawl in at the top. Then get some heavy stones and lay them on the cover to weight down and throw some dead weeds and grass over the pen and triggers and your trap is complete. When the animal tries to enter and sets off the trap by pressing against the long trigger in front, he brings the weighted pole down in the middle of his back, which soon stops his earthly career.

THE PINCH HEAD

This deadfall can also be used at runways without bait. No pen or bait is required. The game will be caught coming from either direction. The trap is "thrown" by the trigger or pushing against it when passing thru. During snowstorms the trap requires considerable attention to keep in perfect working order, but at other

5

times is always in order when placed at runways where it is used without bait.

The trap can also be used at dens without bait with success. If used with bait it should be placed a few feet from the den or near any place frequented by the animal or animals you expect to catch.

Of course we all admit the steel trap is more convenient and up-to-date, says a New Hampshire trapper. You can make your sets faster and can change the steel trap from place to place; of course, the deadfall you cannot. But all this does not signify the deadfall is no good; they are good and when mink trapping the deadfall is good. To the trapper who traps in the same locality every year, when his deadfalls are once built it is only a few minutes' work to put them in shape, then he has got a trap for the season.

I enclose a diagram of a deadfall (called here Log Trap) which, when properly made and baited, there is no such a mink catcher in the trap line yet been devised. This trap requires about an hour to make and for tools a camp hatchet and a good strong jackknife, also a piece of strong string, which all trappers carry.

This trap should be about fifteen inches wide with a pen built with sticks or pieces of boards driven in the ground. (See diagram.) The jaws of this trap consist of two pieces of board three inches wide and about three and a half feet long, resting edgeways one on the other, held firmly by four posts driven in the ground. The top board or drop should move easily up and down before weights are put on. The treddle should be set three inches inside level with the top of bottom board. This is a round stick about three-fourths inch thru, resting against two pegs driven in the ground. (See diagram.) The lever should be the same in size. Now put your stout string around top board. Then set, pass lever thru the string over the cross piece and latch it in front of the treddle. Then put on weights and adjust to spring, heavy or light as desired. This trap should be set around old dams or log jams by the brook, baited with fish, muskrat, rabbit or chicken.

I herewith enclose a drawing of a deadfall that I use for everything up to bear, writes a Rocky Mountain trapper, I hate to acknowledge that I have used it to get "lope" meat with, because I

6

sometimes believe in firing as few shots as I can in some parts of the Mountains.

BOARD OR POLE TRAP

Drawing No. 1 shows it used for bait; a snare can be used on it at the same time by putting the drop or weight where it isn't liable to fall on the animal. Put the weight on the other side of tree or make it fall with the animal to one side. In this case a pole must be strictly used. A good sized rock is all right for small animals. The closer spikes 1 and 2 are together and the longer the tugger end on bottom, the easier it will pull off.

Fig. 1. — Spike driven in tree one-half inch deeper than spike No. 2 (Fig. No. 2) to allow for notch.

3 — Bait on end of trigger.

4 — Heavy rock or log.

5 — Wire, fine soft steel.

6 — Trigger with notch cut in it.

7 — Notch cut in trigger Fig G. Spike No. 2 must have head cut off and pounded flat on end.

7

BAIT SET DEADFALL

In setting it across a trail a peg must be driven in the ground. In this peg the spikes are driven instead of tree as in drawing No. 1. The end of brush stick in between peg and trigger end and when an animal comes either way it will knock the brush and it knocks out the trigger. Good, soft steel wire should be used In setting this deadfall along river bank a stout stick can be driven in bank and hang out over water. This stick will take the place of a limb on tree. One end of a pole held in a slanting position by weighing one end down with a rock will do the same as limb on tree. If a tree is handy and no limb, lean a stout pole up against the tree and cut notches in it for wire to work on.

TRAIL SET DEADFALL

1 — Trail.

2 — Log.

3 — Trigger same as for bait on top deadfall drawing.

4 — Stake driven in ground with spikes driven in it same as above in tree.

5 — Spikes same as above.

6 — Wire.

7 — Tree.

8 — Brush put in trail with one end between trigger and peg to knock off trigger when touched.

This deadfall has never failed me and when trapping in parts of the country where lynx, coyote or wolverine are liable to eat marten in traps, use a snare and it will hang 'em high and out of reach. Snare to be fastened to trigger.

Of course a little pen has to be built when setting this deadfall with bait. In setting in trail it beats any deadfall I have ever used for such animals as have a nature to follow a trail. A fine wire can also be tied to the trigger and stretched across trail instead of a brush and tied on the opposite side of trail. I like it, as the weight can be put high enough from the ground to kill an elk when it drops.

CHAPTER II

BEAR AND COON DEADFALL

I will explain how to make the best bear deadfall, also the best one for coon that ever was made, writes an old and successful deadfall trapper. First get a pole six or eight feet long for bed piece, get another sixteen or eighteen feet long and lay it on top of bed piece. Now drive two stakes, one on each side of bed piece and pole and near one end of bed piece. About 18 or 20 inches from first two stakes drive two more stakes, one on each side of bed piece and fall pole. Now drive two more stakes directly in front of your two back stakes and about two inches in front.

Next cut a stick long enough to come just to the outside of last two stakes driven. Then whittle the ends off square so it will work easy between the treadle stakes and the two inside stakes that your fall works in; next raise your fall pole about three feet high. Get a stick about one inch thru, cut it so that it will be long enough to rest against your treadle and that short stick is your treadle when it is raised above the bed a piece, cut the end off slanting so it will fit against the treadle good.

BEAR OR COON DEADFALL

Slant the other end so the fall pole will fit good. Now five or six inches from the top of the slanted stick cut a notch in your slanted stick. Go to the back side, lift your pole up, set the post on the bed piece. Place the top of the slanted stick against the fall pole. Then place the pole off post in the notch in slant stick. Press back on bottom of slanted stick and place your treadle against the stick. Your trap is set. Make V shape on inside of treadle by driving stakes in the ground, cedar or pine, and hedge it in tight all around. If such there is not, make it as tight as you can. Cover the top tight, the cubby should be 3 feet long, 3 feet high and wide as your treadle stakes.

Stake the bait near the back end of cubby. Be sure the treadle is just above the bed piece. Take the pole off the cubby to set the trap as you have set it from this side. You can set it heavy or light by regulating the treadle. I sometimes drive spikes in the bed piece and file them off sharp as it will hold better. You can weight the fall poles as much as you like after it is set. Don't you see, boys, that the old fellow comes along and to go in he surely will step on the treadle. Bang, it was lowered and you have got him.

This is the best coon deadfall I ever saw. The fall pole for coon should be about 14 inches high when set. Set it under trees or along brooks where you can see coon signs. Bait with frogs, crabs or fish, a piece of muskrat or duck for coon. Build it much the same as for bear, only much smaller. You will find this a successful trap.

I will describe a deadfall for bear which I use, and which works the best of any I have tried, says a Montana trapper. I have two small trees about 30 inches apart, cut a pole 10 feet long for a bed piece and place in front of trees then cut a notch in each tree about 27 inches above the bed piece, and nail a good, strong piece across from one tree to the other in the notches. Cut a long pole five or six inches through for the deadfall, place the large end on top of bed log, letting end stick by the tree far enough to place on poles for weights.

Then cut two stakes and drive on outside of both poles, and fasten top of stakes to the trees one foot above the cross piece. Then on the inside, 30 inches from the trees, drive two more solid stakes about 2 feet apart and nail a piece across them 6 inches lower than the cross piece between the trees. Then cut a lever about three feet long and flatten one end, and a bait stick about two feet long. Cut two notches 6 inches apart, one square on the top and the other on the bottom, and both close to the top end of bait stick.

Fasten bait on the other end and then raise up the deadfall, place the lever stick across the stick nailed between the two trees, letting the end run six inches under the deadfall. Take the bait stick and hook lower notch on the piece nailed on the two stakes and place end of lever in the top notch, then cut weights and place on each side until you think you have enough to hold any bear. Then put on as many more and it will be about right. Stand up old chunks around the sides and back and lots of green brush on the outside. Get it so he can't see the bait.

It doesn't require a very solid pen. I drive about three short stakes in front and leave them one foot high, so when he pulls back they will come against him, and the set is complete. You can weight it with a ton of poles and still it will spring easy. The closer together the two notches the easier it will spring.

This trap can be built lighter and is good for coon. In fact, will catch other fur bearers, but is not especially recommended for small animals, such as ermine and mink.

CHAPTER III

OTTER DEADFALLS

At the present day when steel traps are so cheap and abundant it may sound very primitive and an uncertain way of trapping these animals for one to advocate the use of the deadfall, especially as every hunter knows the animal is much more at home in the water than on land. But on land they go and it was by deadfalls the way-back Indians killed a many that were in their packs at the end of the hunting season.

Of course these wooden traps were not set at haphazard thru the brush as marten traps, but were set up at the otter slide places, and where they crossed points in river bends, or it might be where a narrow strip of land connected two lakes. These places were known from one generation to another and the old traps were freshened up spring and fall by some member of the family hunting those grounds.

These special deadfalls were called otter traps, but really when once set were open for most any animal of a medium size passing that path. The writer has known beaver, lynx, fox and in one instance a cub bear to be caught in one of these deadfalls. There was a simplicity and usefulness about these traps that commended them to the trapper and even now in this rush century some hunters might use them with advantage.

When once set, they remain so until some animal comes along and is caught. I say "caught" because if properly erected they rarely miss. They require no bait and therefore are never out of order by the depredations of mice, squirrels or moose birds. I knew a man who caught two otters together. This may sound fishy, but when once a present generation trapper sees one of these traps set he will readily believe this apparently impossible result is quite likely to happen.

The trap is made thus: Cut four forked young birch about five feet long, pointing the lower ends and leaving the forks uppermost. Plant two of these firmly in the ground at each side of the otter path, three inches apart between them and about twenty inches across the path. These must be driven very hard in the ground and a throat piece put in level between the uprights across the path from side to side. As a choker and to support the weight of logs to kill the otter, cut a pole (tamarac preferable) long enough to pass three feet each side of your picket or uprights, see that this falls easy and clear.

DEAD FALL
FOR
OTTER

OTTER DEADFALL

Now cut two short poles for the forks to lay in from side to side of the path, being in the same direction as the choker. At the middle of one of these short poles tie a good stout cord or rope (the Indians used split young roots), making a loop of same long enough to lay over the pole in front and down to the height the choke pole is going to be. When set, next comes the trigger which must be of hard wood and about a foot long, round at one end and flat at the other. A groove is hacked out all around the stick at the round end. This is to tie the cord to.

The choke stick is now brought up to say twenty inches from

15

the ground and rested on top of the trigger. A stick about an inch in diameter is placed outside the pickets and the flat end of the trigger is laid in against this. The tied stick to be about eight inches from the ground. The tying at the end of the trigger being at one side will create a kind of leverage sufficiently strong to press hard against the tied stick. Care must be taken, however, to have this pressure strong enough but not too strong for the animal to set off.

Now load each end of the choke stick with small laps of wood to insure holding whatever may catch. A little loose moss or grass is placed fluffy under tread stick when set to insure the otter going over and not under. When he clambers over the tread stick his weight depresses it, the trigger flies up, letting the loaded bar fall on his body, which holds him till death.

While my description of the making of a deadfall for otters is plain enough to me, yet the novice may not succeed in constructing one the first time. Still if he is a trapper he will very soon perceive where any mistake may be and correct it. I have used both steel traps and deadfalls and altho I do not wish to start a controversy yet I must say that a deadfall well set is a good trap. For marten on a stump they are never covered unless with snow, nor is the marten when caught destroyed by mice.

Of course, to set a deadfall for otter it must be done in the fall before the ground is frozen. Once made, however, it can be set up either spring or fall and will, with a little repairs, last for years. I am aware the tendency of the age is to progress and not to use obsolete methods, still even some old things have their advantages. Good points are not to be sneered at and one of these I maintain for spring and fall trapping in a district where otter move about from lake to lake or river to river is the old time Indian deadfall.

CHAPTER IV

MARTEN DEADFALL

Having seen a good many descriptions of deadfalls in the H-T-T lately, writes a Colorado trapper, I thought I would try to show the kind that is used around here for marten. It is easily made, and can always be kept above the snow.

First, cut a pole (z) five or six inches through and twelve feet long, lay it in the crotch of a tree five feet from the ground. Then cut two sticks two inches through and fifteen inches long, cut a notch in each three inches from the top and have the notch in one slant downwards (B), the other upwards (A). The sticks should be nailed on each side of the pole (z), the top of which should be flattened a little. Have the notches about six inches above the top of the pole.

Cut another stick 10 inches long (F), cut the top off square and nail it six inches farther down the pole on the same side as (B), have the top five inches above the top of pole (Z). Now cut two more sticks two and one-half feet long (C-D), cut a notch in each two inches from the top and nail a stick (E) across them in the notches, so they will be about seven inches apart. Set a straddle of the pole (Z); they should be two inches farther down the pole than (F). Then cut another pole (X) ten feet long, lay it under (Z), lift up one end of it and nail the stick C and D to each side of it. See that when the sticks C, D and E are lifted up they will fall clear and easily.

Now cut a bait stick (G) one-half inch through and seven inches long, sharpened at one end. Cut another stick (H) an inch through and fifteen inches long, flatten a little on one side. To set the trap lift up C, D, E and X, and put the end of H under E and rest it on the top of F, hold down the other end while you put the bait stick (G) in the notches A and B, then let the end of H come up on the outside of B against the end of G. Put the bait on the other end of G; when the end is pulled out of the notch the trap will spring and spring easily if made properly. Lay a block of wood at the back end and

17

some small sticks on top, so the animal will have to crawl under E to get the bait. Muskrat makes the best bait for marten.

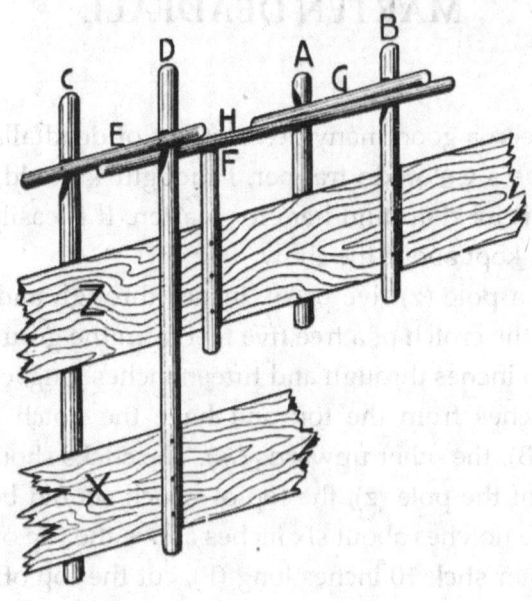

MARTEN DEADFALL

When you find a tall straight spruce or something that is pretty straight (not a balsam) cut it about a foot over your head, says a Northwestern trapper, or as high as you can. When you have cut it, split the stump down the center two feet. Be careful doing this, for you are striking a dangerous blow as I have good cause to know and remember. Trim out the tree clean and taper off the butt end to make it enter into split. Drive down into split about fourteen inches. Cut a crotch into ground or snow solid.

Now cut the mate of this piece already in, split and put into split and into crotch on top of other. Have the piece heavy enough to hold wolverine. See cuts for the rest. Cover bait as shown in cut. I do not make my trip sticks the same as others, but I am afraid that I cannot explain it to you. See cuts for this also. Use your own judgment. Of course you will sometimes find it is not necessary to go to all this bother. For instance, sometimes you will find a natural hanger for your trap. Then you don't have to have the long peg or pole to hold it stiff.

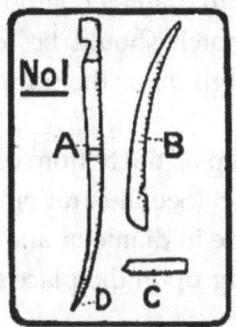 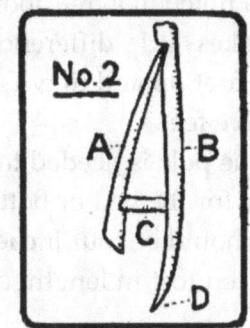

MARTEN TRAP TRIGGERS

This trap is used heavy enough by some "long line" trappers for wolverine. They blacken bait and cover as shown in No. 4. In the two small illustrations the triggers are shown in No. 1 separate and in No. 2 set. A is the bait and trip stick, B the lever, C is the upright. B in No. 1 is where the bait should be.

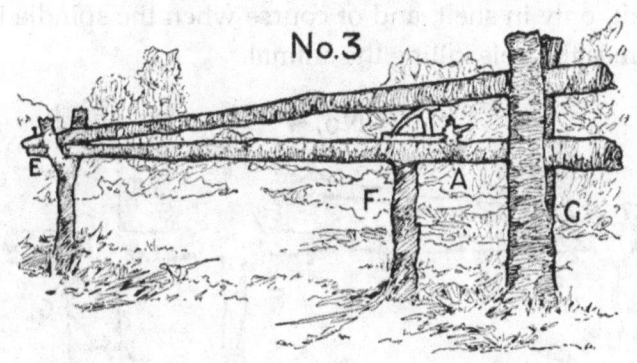

ANOTHER MARTEN DEADFALL

In No. 3 A is bait, E is pin which fastens deadfall to under pole and prevents deadfall from turning to one side. F is post to keep under pole from bending.

In No. 4 HH are nails which fasten down a springy piece of wood to keep cover over bait. Cover with fir or spruce boughs.

Another deadfall much used by marten trappers is constructed by cutting a notch in a tree about a foot in diameter, altho the size of the tree makes little difference. The notch should be four inches deep and a foot up and down and as high up as the trapper can cut — four or five feet.

Only one pole is needed for this trap as the bottom of the notch cut answers for the bed or bottom piece. (See illustration.) The pole for the fall should be four inches or more in diameter and anywhere from six to ten feet in length, depending upon the place selected to set.

The end fartherest from the bait or notched tree must be as high as the notch. This can be done by driving a forked stake into the ground or by tying that end of the pole to a small tree if there is one growing at the right place.

If the pole for the fall is larger than the notch is deep, the end must be flattened so that it will work easy in the notch, as a piece of wood has been nailed over the notch to hold the fall pole in place.

The triggers used are generally the figure 4 and set with bait pointing as shown. There is no place for the marten to stand while eating bait, only in shelf, and of course when the spindle is pulled, down comes the pole killing the animal.

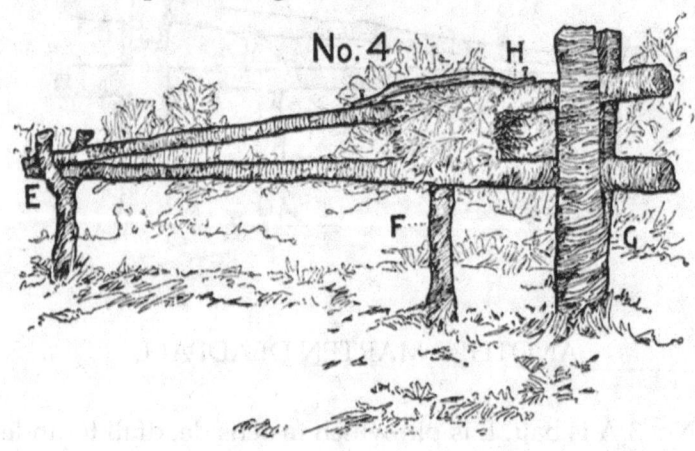

HIGH BUILT MARTEN DEADFALL

TREE DEADFALL

This shelf protects the bait and bed piece and the snow does not fill in between and require so much attention as the one first described.

This deadfall may also be built on a stump with a small enclosure or pen and the two-piece trigger used. Most trappers place the bait or long trigger on bottom pole, when trapping for marten. It will be readily seen that a marten, to get the bait, will stand between the "fall" and bed or under pole and of course is caught while trying to get the bait.

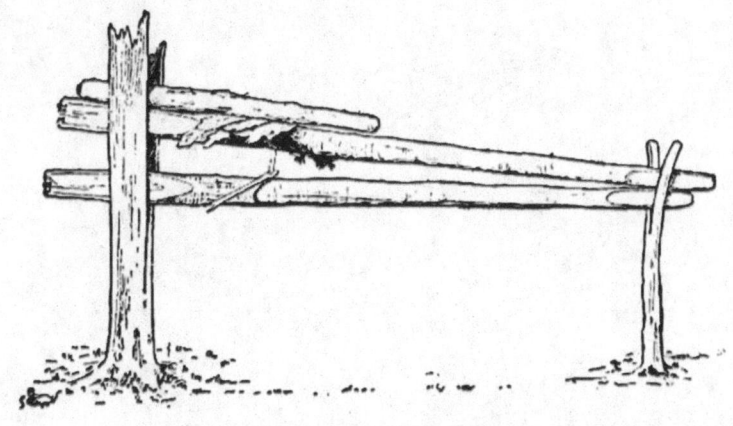

MORE MARTEN TRAP TRIGGERS

The height that deadfalls for marten should be built depends upon how deep the snow gets. In the fall and early winter they can be built on the ground or logs and other fur-bearers are taken as well.

A few inches of snow will not interfere with the workings of deadfalls on the ground, but deep snows will. To make catches the trapper must clean out under the fall pole each round. This is no small task. The trapper is always on the lookout for suitable places to construct Marten deadfalls.

When the snows get several feet deep, and the trapper makes his rounds on snowshoes, the deadfalls constructed several feet above the ground are the ones that make the catches.

CHAPTER V

STONE DEADFALLS

The stone deadfall here described is used by trappers wherever flat stones can be found and is a good trap to catch skunk, opossum, mink and other small game in. The trap is made as follows:

The figure 4 trigger is best for this trap and is made after this manner: standard (1) is made by cutting a stick five or six inches long out of hard wood and whittling it to a flat point, but blunt at one end; (2) is about five inches long with a notch cut within about one and one-half inches of the end with the other end made square so that it will fit in (3) which is the bait stick. This is only a straight stick sixteen or eighteen inches long, while the other end of the stick should have a small prong on it, a tack driven in, or something to hold the bait in position. The best way will be to tie the bait on also.

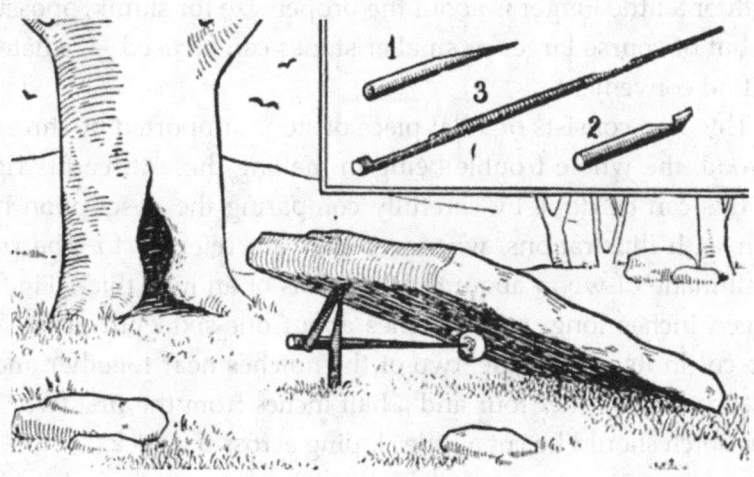

FLAT STONE TRAP

After you have found a flat stone weighing from 50 to 100 pounds, depending upon what game you expect to trap, select the place for the trap, first place a small flat stone underneath so that your game will be killed quicker and also so that the upright trigger will not sink into the ground. Lift up the large, or upper stone, kneeling on one knee before the stone resting the weight of the stone on the other. This leaves both hands free to set the trap. This is done by placing the triggers in the position shown in illustration and then letting the stone down very easily on the triggers. You should keep your knee under the stone all the time until you see that it comes down easily and does not "go off" of its own weight. The bait should always be put on before the trap is set. This trap will go off easy and you must be careful that the bait you put on is not too heavy and will cause the trap to fall of its own accord.

This trap can be made to catch rabbits which will come in handy to bait other traps for larger game. In trapping for rabbits bait with apples, cabbage, etc.

This trap does not take long to make, as no pen need be built, the top stone is large enough to strike the animal, making no difference in what position it gets when after the bait. A stone two or three inches thick and say thirty inches across and the same length or a little longer is about the proper size for skunk, opossum, etc., but of course larger or smaller stones can be used — whatever you find convenient.

This trap consists of a flat piece of stone supported by three fits of wood, the whole trouble being in making these three fits right, and this can be done by carefully comparing the description here given with illustrations, whenever they are referred to. The parts are all made of wood about three-eighths of an inch thick. Fig. 1 is thirteen inches long, with notches about one-sixteenth of an inch deep cut in its upper side, two of the notches near together and at one end, and another four and a half inches from the first two. The latter notch should be cut a little sloping across the stick.

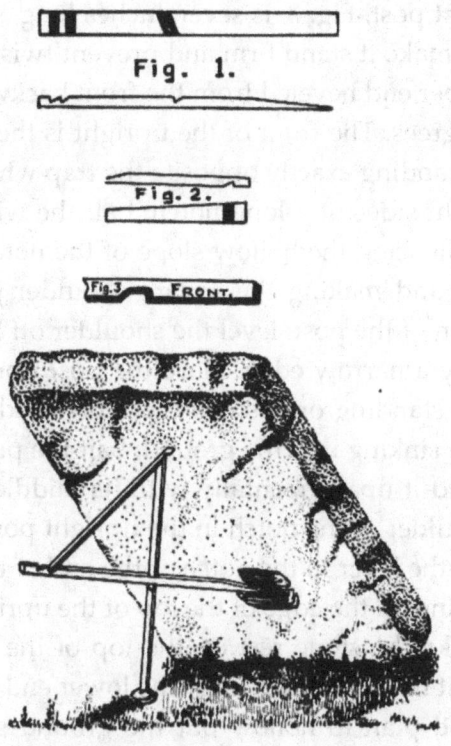

Fig. 1.

Fig. 2.

Fig.3 **FRONT.**

STONE DEADFALL TRIGGERS

Figure 1 represents a top view and the piece next below it is a side view of the piece of wood as it should be made, and end fartherest from the notches being trimmed to a point to hold the bait. This constitutes the trigger.

The lever is shown in Fig. 2, the cut above giving a side view and that below it a bottom view of this part of the trap. The piece of wood needed for it is six and one-half inches long, one inch wide at one end, and tapering down to three-sixteenths of an inch at the other; a notch is cut across the under side one and a half inches from the wide end. Level off the upper side of the narrow end to about one-half the original thickness. If the flat stone to be used is a heavy one, the notch must not be more than 1 inch from the end; otherwise the leverage on the notches would be greater than is desirable, tending to hold the parts together too rigidly.

The upright post, Fig. 3, is seven inches long, slightly forked at the bottom (to make it stand firm and prevent twisting round when in use), the upper end beveled from the front backwards at an angle of about 45 degrees. The front of the upright is the side that would face a person standing exactly opposite the trap when set.

On the right side cut a long notch, half the width of the wood in depth, commencing the hollow slope of the notch one inch from the lower end and making the square shoulder just three inches from the bottom of the post; level the shoulder off from the front so as to leave only a narrow edge. Place the post upright, (see Fig. 4) it's forked end standing on a small piece of wood or flat stone, to prevent it from sinking into the ground; bait the pointed end of the trigger and hold it up horizontally with its middle notch, catching behind the shoulder of the notch in the upright post; then place the beveled end of the lever in the notch at the end of trigger, the notch in the lever laying on the edge of the top of the upright post.

Lastly, make the stone rest on the top of the lever, arranging the stone so that the bait will be near the lower end of the stone.

It is a good plan to hollow out the ground somewhat under where the stone falls, to allow a space for the pieces of the Fig. 4 to lay without danger of being broken. The bait, also, should be something that will flatten easily and not hard enough to tilt the stone up after it has fallen.

The trouble with most deadfalls usually set, is in the weight of stone. When you get one heavy enough it will not trip easy when game takes hold, and oftentimes break head piece where the head takes hold of standard. The head piece from stone down to where standard sets in notch should be fully 2 1/4 inches, so when stone starts to fall it throws triggers out from under; otherwise, stone will catch and break them.

26

THE INVITATION — SKUNK

Young trappers when you are making triggers preparatory for your sets, tie each pair together separately as they are finished, then when you are ready to set there are no misfits. Now we are up to the bait stick. It should under no condition, be more than 9 inches long, and oftentimes shorter will answer better. A slotted notch on one end the width of triggers, and sharpened at the other, is all that is necessary. Then the bait will lay on the foundation of trap within 5 or 6 inches of front of the trap. Don't put bait away back under stone. You loose all the force when it falls.

In building foundations for traps the utmost caution should be exercised in getting them good and solid. (See how well you can do it instead of how quick.) Begin in the fall before the trapping season is on, locate and build your trap, and be sure the top stone is plenty heavy, raise it up and let it fall several times. If it comes together with the bang of a wolf trap and will pinch a hair, so much the better.

To illustrate: While squirrel shooting one morning in the fall of 1905, I was standing on a ledge where I used to trap for coons, and I happened to remember of a trap underneath me. I just thought I would see if it was there. I went down and kicked away the drifted leaves and found it intact and ready for business. When I lifted it up the foundation was as solid as the day I put it there, and that was in the fall of 1890, and I want to say right here that it took all the strength I had to set it.

KILLED WITHOUT SCENTING

Trappers, if you will try one or more of the above described deadfalls for those skunk, I think you can tie their pelts about your neck for protection cold mornings, and none will be the wiser as far as smell goes, provided, however, you put some obstruction to the right and left of the trap so it will compel his skunkship to enter direct in front, and then carefully adjust the length of bait stick so stone will crush him about the heart. I have taken quite a lot of skunk and very few ever scented where the head and heart were under stone, writes an Ohio trapper.

I always had a preference for above described traps for many reasons, yet if you live where there is no stone, you are not in it.

Deadfalls come in handy sometimes and with no cost whatever — unless the cost is building them. Will send two illustrations of the stone deadfalls writes a successful deadfall trapper. Will say that there is a right and a wrong way to set the deadfall. If you want to make sure of your catch never set your deadfall flat with short triggers shaped like figure 4, but make long triggers instead and have the weight or choker sit almost upright and draw the top trigger close to the one that it rests on at the bottom. In this way you have a trap that will be very easy to touch off.

The way that some set their deadfalls the animal can remove bait without being caught, simply because they draw the bait out from under the trap and stand far enough away to be out of danger of being caught. I can take a two hundred pound weight and set a deadfall that will catch a small field mouse but it would not do to have them knock that easy for you will get game that is too small to handle.

THE RIGHT WAY

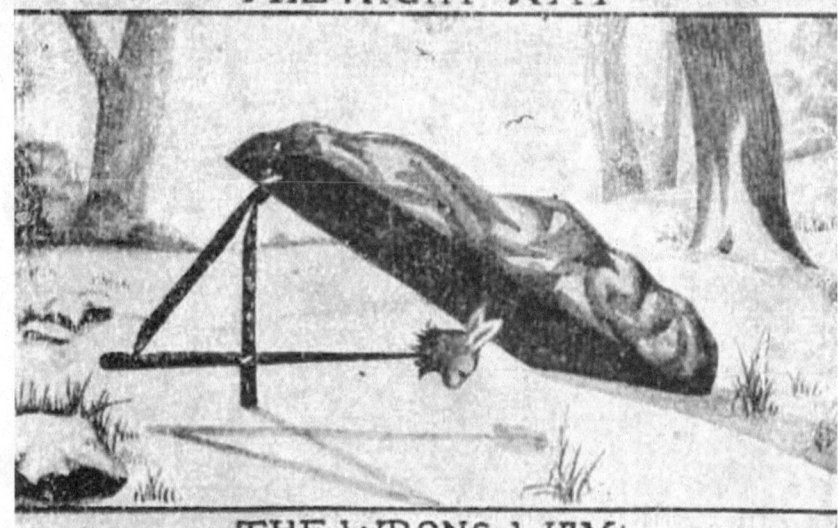

THE WRONG WAY

RIGHT AND WRONG WAY

CHAPTER VI

THE BEAR PEN

I will give a description of a bear pen, writes a Canadian trapper. The bottom of the floor is made first of two logs about (1-1) nine feet long and nine or ten inches thick. They are placed side by side as shown in cut and two other logs (2-2) nine feet long and eighteen inches in thickness are placed one on each side of the bottom logs. Then cut two short logs about twelve or fourteen inches thick and long enough to reach across the pen and extend about six inches over each side. Notch these down, as shown in cut (3-3) so that the top of the logs are about three or four inches higher than the sides.

Cut notches in the top of these logs so that when logs 4-4 will lay solid on top of the other side logs. If they don't lie solid enough bore holes in the ends of the short logs and drive wooden pins in the holes. The top of the short logs and the inside of the long logs should be flattened and a short block (5) fitted loosely in one end, and the other end should be closed by a block driven down in notches cut in the sides of 4-4, as shown in small cut. The top of the block (6) should be about five inches lower than the top of the side logs. Notches are next cut in the side logs, directly over this block, so that when the roller (7) is in place, it will fit down snugly on this block. The roller is about five inches thick and should turn easily in the notches.

Rear end view of Trap.

BEAR PEN TRAP

31

The next step is to make the lid. It should be made of two logs of such a size that they will entirely close the top of the trap. They are notches down and pinned onto the roller and block 5. These logs should project over rear end of pen about four or five feet. Before pinning these logs in places, a hole should be made for the bait stick, half of it being cut in each log. Pins should be driven in the side logs, over the roller, so that the bear cannot raise the lid. Two crotches are then cut and set up at the sides of the trap and spiked solid to the sides. A short pole is then placed in the crotches and a long pole, running lengthwise of the trap, is fastened to the lid at one end with wire and the other ends fits into a notch in the bait stick when the trap is set. The bait stick has a spike driven thru it on the inside of the trap to keep it from pulling thru.

To set the trap, pile stones on the end of the lid until it will tip easily, then put a pole thru under lid and go inside and fasten the bait on the bait stick. Then pull the long pole down and hook it into the notch in the bait stick. Remove the stones from lid and take the pole from under it and the trap is set and ready for the first bear that comes along. If the lid does not seem heavy enough, pile stone on it. A trap of this kind may be made by two men in half a day and will be good for a number of years.

The log trap is one of the very best methods of taking the bear, it beats the deadfall all to nothing, says an old and experienced Ohio bear trapper. It is a sure shot every time; I have never known it to fail except where the pen had stood for a number of years and become rotten. In a case of that kind the bear would have no difficulty in gnawing his way out. This trap or pen, as I shall call it, has been time tried and bear tested. My father used to make these traps and many is the time when a boy I have ridden on horseback upon a narrow path, cut for the purpose of letting a horse pass along and on nearing the pen heard the growling and tearing around of the bear in the pen and the hair on my head would almost crowd my hat off.

Go about building it this way: First select the spot where you have reason to believe that bear inhabit; now having made your selection, get a level place and on this spot lay a course of logs with the top flattened off; this may be eight by three feet. This being done, commence to lay up the house of logs six to eight inches in diameter. Three sides of each log should be flattened; these will be the top, bottom and the inside. It is necessary this be done, for they must fit closely together in order that the bear cannot get a starting place to gnaw. This is why I suggest that the inside of the log be flattened. It is a well-known fact that you can put any gnawing animal into a square box and he cannot gnaw out for he cannot get the starting point.

Lay a short log first, then a long one, notching each corner as you go so the logs will fit closely together. Now for the front corners; drive a flattened stake into the ground, letting the flattened side come against the logs. Now as you proceed to lay on a course of logs pin thru the stake into each log. Now go on up until you get a height of about four feet, then lay on, for the top, a course of short logs commencing at the back end.

Between the second and third logs cut out a little notch and flatten the under side of this log around the notch; this is to receive the trigger, which is made of a small pole about three inches thick. Put this into the hole and let it come down within ten inches of the floor. Then cut a notch in the side facing the front of the pen and so it will fit up against the under side of the leg with the notch in; now you may make a notch in the trigger about six inches above the top of the pen and on the same side of the trigger that the first notch was made. Now the trigger is ready except adjusting the bait.

Next lay a binder on top of the pen and upon either end of the short course of logs; pin the binders at either end so the bear cannot raise the top off the pen. You may also lay on three or four logs to weight it down and make it doubly sure. You may pin the first short top log in front to the side logs to keep the front of the pen from spreading. Now we have the body of the pen complete.

The door is the next thing in order. The first or bottom log ought to be twelve feet long, but it is not necessary for the balance of them to be that length; flatten the top and bottom of each log so they will lie tight together, also flatten off the inside of the door so it will work smoothly against the end of the pen. Lay the logs of the door onto the first or long log, putting a pin in each end of the logs as you lay them on. Go on this way until you have enough to reach the height of the pen and fully cover the opening.

BEAR ENTERING PEN

Another way of fastening the door together is to get the logs all ready, then lay them upon the ground and pin two pieces across the door. Either way will do. Now the door being in readiness, put it in its place and drive two stakes in the ground to keep the animal from shoving the door away. If these do not appear to be solid enough to support the door against an onslaught, you may cut a notch in the outside of the stake near the top; get a pole eight feet in length, sharpen the ends, letting one end come in the notch of the stake and the other into the ground; this will hold the door perfectly solid. Cut a slight notch in the top log of the door for the end of the spindle and the next move is to raise the door to the

34

proper height. Set a stud under the door to keep it from falling. Get your spindle ready, flatten the top of either end a little, then cut a stanchion just the right length to set under the spindle on the first top log.

Tie your bait onto the lower end of the trigger, one man going inside to put the trigger in the proper place. To facilitate the springing of the trap, lay a small round stick in the upper notch of the trigger, letting the end of the spindle come up under the stick and as the bear gets hold of the meat on the bottom of the trigger the least pull will roll the trigger from the end of the spindle. However, it will spring very easily as the stanchion under the end of the spindle is so near the end.

This kind of trap can be made by two men in one day or less, and it often happens that the hunter and trapper wants to set a trap for bear a long way from any settlement or road. The carrying of a fifty pound bear trap a distance of twenty or thirty miles is no little task. Then again, this trap costs nothing but a little time and the trapper's whole life is given over to time. One man can make this trap alone and set it, but it is better for two to work together in this work, for in case the door should spring upon him while he was inside he would be forever lost. I have caught two wildcats at once in this pen, but it is not to be expected that you will get more than one bear or other large animal at a time.

CHAPTER VII

PORTABLE TRAPS

In describing a portable deadfall, an Indiana trapper writes as follows: We took a piece of sawed stuff 2 x 4, say 5 feet long, then another the same size and length. For upright pieces to hold the main pieces so one would fall square on the other, we used sawed stuff 1 x 3, two pieces set straight up and down at each end, or about far enough to leave the back end stick out three inches, and front end or end where the triggers set, 6 inches.

Nail these 1 x 3 two on each end as directed above, nail to lower piece 2 x 4 only, then at back end bore a hole through the two uprights and also upper 2 x 4, or the piece that falls, put a bolt through, or a wood pin if the hole in the 2 x 4 is larger than those through the uprights; then you are ready to raise it up and let it "drop" to see whether it works smoothly or not.

Better nail a block 2 x 4 between the tops of the uprights to keep them from spreading apart, then it is ready all except the triggers and string for them to run against. It is portable, you can pick it up and move it anywhere, only a stake or two needed driven down on each side. Where string is shown as tied to little bush should be a small stake.

DEN SET DEADFALL

"SHEAR TRAP"

I send a drawing of a trap called the "Shear Trap," writes an Eastern trapper. This is not a new trap, neither is it my own invention. I have used this style and can recommend it to be O. K., cheap, easy made, light to move, will last and will catch most any small animal.

This trap is made as follows: Take 4 strips of board 4 feet 4 inches long, by 3 inches wide. Bore one inch hole two inches from end of all four of them. Now make two rounds about 13 inches long and put two of the boards on each side of the round. At the other end put the two middle boards on the other round (see illustration). Make one other round fifteen inches long, same size as the others. Put the two outside boards on it, forming two separate frames at the other end — so the two inside boards can turn on the round to which they are coupled.

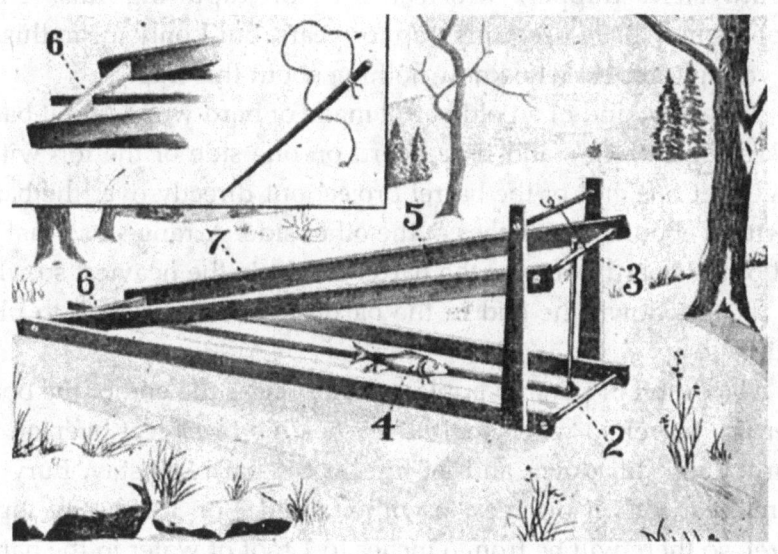

PORTABLE WOODEN TRAP

Take two strips three inches wide, two feet and six inches long. Bore one inch hole two inches from the top end and put round broom stick thru it seventeen inches long. Fasten all the rounds by wedges or small wooden pins. Stand the two strips last mentioned on the outside of the frame at the end they separate and make them fast so as to stand perpendicular. For bait stick take lathe or one-half inch board one inch wide. Bore hole as shown in cut (figure 6) cut notch (figure 2). For trigger any stick 18 inches long, 5/8 inch thick will do: tie string 2 inches from end and tie other end at figure 1, pass the short end under round from the outside (figure 3) and catch in notch in bait lath (figure 2), the other end bait at figure 4. Put weight at figure 5. Cover trap at figure 6 to keep animal from going in from back up to figure 7. For bait I use fresh fish, muskrat, bird, etc., and scent with honey or blood.

THE BARREL TRAP

I promised in my last letter to describe the barrel trap, says a Northwestern trapper, which I use for capturing rats. Other trappers may have used this trap for years, but I only mean this for the young trappers who know nothing about this trap.

Take any kind of an old barrel made of hard wood (a salt barrel makes a good one), and fix a board on one side of the top with a hinge. Let one end of the barrel project out directly over the barrel to within about 5 or 6 inches of the other side. Arrange it so that the end of the board not over the barrel is a little the heaviest so when the rat tilts down the end in the barrel it will come back to place again.

Place a bit of parsnip apple, or celery near the end of the board over the barrel so when the rat reaches his front feet over on the board it will tilt down and let him in the barrel to stay. Bury the barrel near a river or creek to within about 2 or 3 inches of top of barrel, so there will be from 6 inches to 1 foot of water in the barrel. If there is much water in the barrel the most of the rats will be dead when you visit your traps. Several may be captured in one night in this kind of a trap.

BLOCK TRAP

Saw a small log in blocks from 4 to 6 inches long. Bore an inch hole through the center. Take nails and drive them so that they form a "muzzle" in one end and have the nails very sharp. Fasten your blocks with a piece of wire and put it in the runway or on a log or anywhere that a coon will see it, and nine out of ten will put his foot into it. I bait with honey. I caught 75 or 80 coons this season with "block" snares.

I put stoppers or false bottoms in one end of the block, piece of corn cob or anything will do. Cut the foot off to get the animal out of this snare.

The illustration shows a square block with the hole bored in the side. This is done to better show how it should be done, although when set, the hole should be up. Bait with a piece of fresh rabbit, frog, or anything that coon are fond of.

Instead of the blocks the auger hole can be bored in a log or root of a tree if a suitable one can be found where coon frequent.

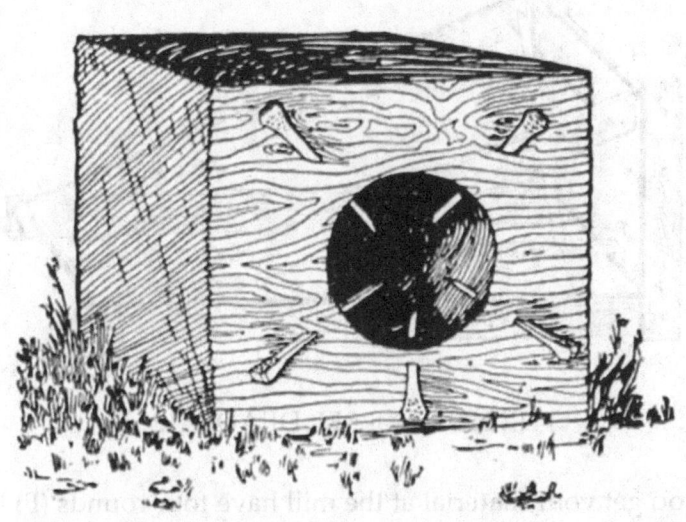

THE BLOCK TRAP

THE "NOXEMALL" DEADFALL

The best material is spruce, but if spruce is not to be had, hard wood is better than soft. Follow directions closely; never use old, dozy wood; good, sound, straight-grained material is the cheapest to use. A good way to get your material is to go to the saw-mill, select good straight-grained 2 x 4 studding, have them ripped lengthwise again, making four strips out of the original 2 x 4, each strip being two inches wide by one inch thick; then have them cut in the lengths — two standards (A), 14 inches long; (B) two side pieces, 2 1/2 feet long; (C) two drop bars, 2 1/2 feet. Bore a hole in each piece with a one inch bit, two inches from the end of the piece to the center of the hole. (D) A piece of lath about 8 inches long, with one end beveled off to fit in slot of E; tie a piece of small rope, about a foot long, two inches from the other end. (E) A piece of lath, 2 1/2 feet long, with a slot cut crosswise two inches from one end and a piece of rope tied two inch from the other end, about a foot long.

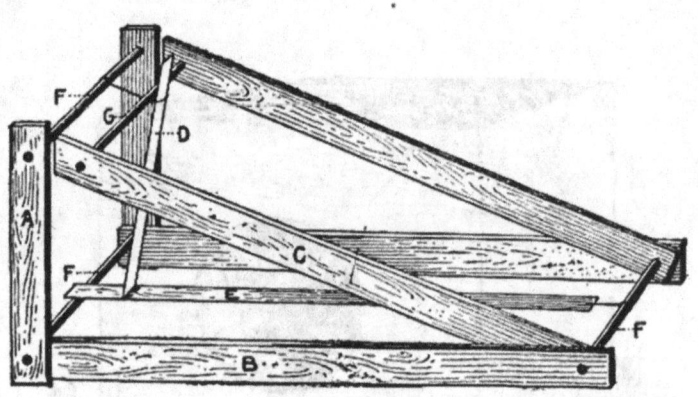

THE NOX-EM-ALL DEADFALL

If you get your material at the mill have four rounds (F) turned out of oak or maple (must be hard wood), three of them being 12 inches long, one being 8 inches long, 7/8 inch in diameter. They must be some smaller than the hole, as they swell when wet.

Your trap is now ready to put together. Take one 12 inch round slip on the side pieces B first, then the two standards A; next place a 12 inch round in the holes in the top of the standards. The front end of the trap is done, except fastening the standards to the round and the setting apparatus to the top round of standards. Next take the remaining 12 inch round slip on the drop bars C first, then the side pieces B outside; next place the short round G in the front end of drop bar C.

You can drive nails thru the outside pieces and the round. Where there are two pieces on a side on one round, fasten thru the outside piece, always leaving the inside piece loose so that it will turn on the round. A much better way, altho it is more work, is to bore a hole thru the side piece and round and drive in a hard wood plug. This is the best way, because if any part of the trap breaks you can knock out the plug much easier than to pull out a nail. The holes should be bored with a 1/4 inch bit.

Tie the rope attached to E to the rear round, leaving two inches play, between E and the round. Tie the rope attached to D to the top round of standards, leaving two inches play at top and two inches between lower end of D and bottom round.

First place a stone on the drop bar, weighing 20 pounds. Then raise the drop bar high enough so that you can place the short lath under the round of drop so that the weight rests on the rope. These is the secret of setting. The pressure on top forces the lower end to fly up. Now place the beveled end of the short lath in the slot of the long lath and the trap is set.

Hang your bait from the drop bars, under the weight, about eight inches from the front. The game will then come to the side of the trap. Never tie bait on the lath.

Set the trap in front of the hole, block up by setting up two stones V shape on the upper side of hole, forcing game thru the trap to enter or come out.

CHAPTER VIII

SOME TRIGGERS

During my trapping experiences I remember of visiting an old trapper's deadfalls and at that time I had never seen or used any trigger other than the figure 4, but this trapper used the prop and spindle. I looked at several of his traps; in fact, went considerably out of my way to look at some eight or ten of them. Two of these contained game — a skunk and opossum. I had often heard of these triggers, but was skeptical about them being much good. I now saw that these triggers were all right and on visiting my traps again set a few of them with these triggers. Since that time I have never used the figure 4.

The prop and spindle I know will look to many too hard to "go off," but they can be set so that they will go off fairly easy. It is not necessary that the trap be set so that the least touch will make it go off. It is best to have the trap set so that mice nibbling at bait will not throw it.

Trappers who have never used the deadfall will, no doubt, find that after they use them a short time and become better acquainted with their construction and operation that they will catch more game than at first. This is only natural as all must learn from experience largely, whether at trapping or anything else.

The prop is a straight piece about seven inches long and about one-half inch in diameter. The spindle, or long trigger, is about the size of the prop, but should be sixteen or eighteen inches long with a prong cut off within two inches of the end to help hold the bait on more securely. See cut elsewhere showing these triggers and of the figure likewise. These illustrations will give a better idea of how the triggers are made to those who have never seen or used them.

I saw some time ago where a brother wanted to know how to make a deadfall, writes an Illinois trapper. I send a picture of one that I think is far ahead of any that I have seen in the H-T-T yet, that is, the triggers. I have seen deadfall triggers that would catch and not fall when the bait was pulled at, but there is no catch to these.

Trigger No. 1 is stub driven in the ground with a notch cut in the upper end for end of bait. Stick No. 5 to fit in No. 3 is another stub driven in ground for bait stick No. 5 to rest on top. No. 3 is a stick, one end laid on top of bait stick outside of stub No. 2, the other end on top of lower pole. No. 4 is the prop stick. One end is set on stick No. 3 about one inch inside the lower pole the other end underneath the upper pole. The X represents the bait. When the bait stick is pulled out of notch in stub No. 1, the upper pole comes down and has got your animal.

ILLINOIS TRAPPER'S TRIGGERS

If you find your bait is caught between the poles you may know the bait is not back in the box far enough. If you find the trap down and bait and bait stick gone, you may know that the bait is too far back. The animal took his whole body in before he pulled the bait.

I have tried to describe this trap for the ones that don't know how to make a deadfall.

Somebody wants to know how to make a good deadfall. Well the plans published in back numbers of H-T-T are all right except the figure four sticks and bait. Make your sticks like this, and you will be pleased with the way they work, says an experienced trapper.

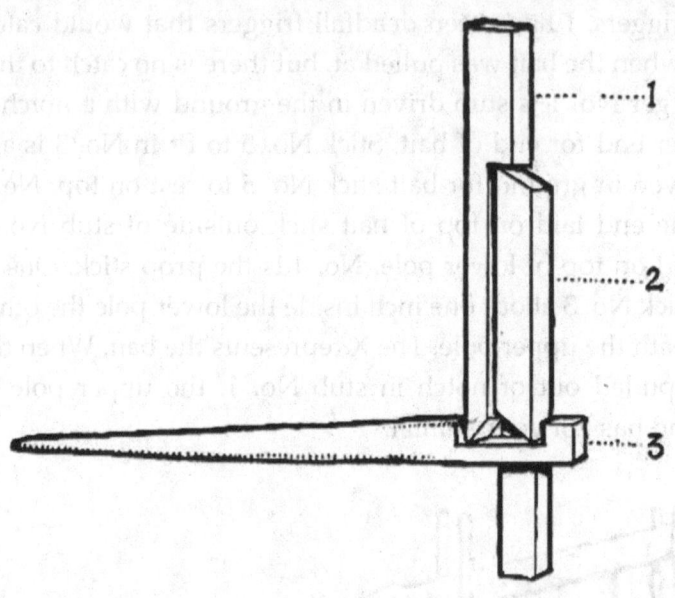

TRIP TRIGGERS

No. 2 flat view. The trigger sets in the slanting cut in side of No. 2. Don't put bait on trigger. Put it in back end of pen and pin it to the ground. Turn trigger across opening slanted slightly in, then you get them by neck or shoulders. The longer the slot in the trigger, the harder they will trip. Set as straight up as possible.

Make 1 and 2 of hard wood. Saw a block 3 1/2 inches long and split into 3/4 inch squares. Make cuts square with a saw and split out the part you don't want. Bevel ends with a hatchet. Make trigger of green hard wood stick with bark on.

I cut a tree from 8 to 10 inches in diameter and cut off 7 feet long. Split the piece open and bury one piece on a level with the earth — split side up — and place the other half on top. I hew off any bumps and make a perfect fit. Then I cut out bushes the size of my arm, and drive them down on each side of my fall and leave them an inch or two higher than I expect my top log to be when set. Be sure to begin far enough at the back to force the animals to go in at the front. I use the figure four triggers and tie the bait to the long trigger.

44

Another trigger is made as follows: Cut two forks and lay pole across just in front of the log on top of the forks. Take another piece of timber about four feet long, tie a string to each end and let one end have a trigger and the other be tied on your top log. I drive a nail in the top log and tie the string to it, and I call this my Fly trigger. It acts as a lever, for when the fly comes up over the piece on the forks and the trigger goes over half way back by the side of the log, and the trigger about a foot long — straight and thin, and sticks under the log — have a short trigger tied to the fly pole and a forked sapling the size of your finger and long enough to stick in the ground to hold the trigger. Put the bait on long trigger and catch the short trigger through the fork and let it catch the long trigger. This trigger leaves the fall open in front and is the one I prefer.

Take two small logs about 10 or 12 feet long, large enough to break a coon's back, and make a pen about midway, or one-third from front end, to put the bait in, and the trigger. Two foot boards, or saplings will do, and make the pen so that the animal will have to step across the bottom log and take the bait, and be sure to set so that the top log will fall across the mink, coon, skunk, or opossum, as they are the animals I kill with the fall. Use fly pole triggers as above, for this deadfall.

I make these falls near the runways of the animals I wish to catch. When I am sure to stay at a place, I build my falls in the summer and by the trapping time they look old and natural.

CHAPTER IX

TRIP TRIGGERS

The deadfall shown here can be used at dens or in paths where animals travel frequently. When set across the entrance of dens it will catch an animal going in without bait. That is, it will catch an animal going in, as the triggers are so constructed that they can only be pushed towards the bait as shown in illustration. If the trap is to be used at dens without bait the regular figure 4 triggers had best be used, but set extending along the log instead of back into the pen. An animal in entering will strike the trigger and down comes the fall.

The trap shown here and the triggers are made as follows: Cut two logs and lay one on the ground. This log should be at least four feet long. Place it firmly on the ground with flat side up. This log need not be as flat as shown in illustration, but should be flattened slightly. Drive two stakes three feet long within a foot or so of one end (8) and (9).

Now come to the other end and drive two more (10) and (11). Stake ten which is directly opposite from (11) you want to be careful not to split, as one of the triggers rests on it. The fall is now placed in position, that is the upper log. The end of this is split and a stake driven in the ground so that the fall will not turn between the stakes but is held firmly. See that the fall will work easily up and down; that the stakes are not so close together that the fall binds, yet it wants to fit snugly.

Cut trip stick (4) and trigger (3), lifting the fall up with one knee and place end of (3) onto (4) slightly, so that a small pressure on (4) will spring the trap. After you have the trap set spring it to see that it works all right. If the trap works all right and you are setting across the entrance of a den the pen of course is not wanted. If you are setting in paths or near dens, drive stakes in a semi-circle as shown in illustration, but the stakes should stick above the ground some eighteen inches or about as high as the "fall" pole when set. It is a good plan to throw leaves or grass on the stakes.

ANIMAL ENTERING TRIP DEADFALL

A small notch (5) should be cut in upright post (8) for trip stick to fit in to hold it up to that end. Be careful, however, that this notch is not cut too deep. The bait (6) is placed back in the pen and fastened with wire or a stake driven thru it into the ground. The open space over bait is now covered over and the entire trap can be made to not look so suspicious by cutting brush and throwing over it excepting in front of the bait. An animal in going in for bait steps on or pushes the long stick (marked 4 at one end and 5 at the other) off of (3) and is usually caught.

This is another good trip trigger deadfall. A short log should be laid on the ground and the two stakes driven opposite each other as in the trap just described. These stakes are not shown, as a better view of the triggers and workings of the trap can be had by omitting these.

In the illustration the "fall" pole is weighted, but it is best to have the pole heavy enough and not weighted. The stakes on which the upper or cross piece is nailed should be from twelve to eighteen inches apart. The cross piece need not be heavy, yet should be strong so that the weight of the fall will not bend it.

TRIP TRIGGER FALL

The pens or enclosures used cannot be covered, as this would interfere with the workings of the triggers. If the pen is sixteen inches or higher very few animals will climb over to get bait, but will go in where the trapper wants and if properly made and set are apt to catch the game.

Along in the late seventies or beginning of the eighties, when a good sized muskrat would bring about as much as a common prime mink, and a steel trap was quite a prize to be in possession of, I had perhaps two dozen traps, some old fashioned, that would be quite a curiosity at present, besides a few Newhouse No. 0 and 1.

That was in Ontario, Canada. Skunk, mink, coon, muskrat and fox were the furs in that part, Waterloo, Brant and Oxford Counties. Later I used this deadfall with success in Iowa and other sections, so that there is no doubt but that it will be found a good fur catcher in most localities.

I used to catch a great deal with deadfalls, — picture of which I here enclose. I have seen nearly all the different makes of deadfalls and have tried some of them, but the one I here send you the picture of, which can be easily understood, is the one I have had the most success with. I believe they are the best, and an animal can't get at the bait without striking it off, besides some animals will examine a bait without touching it. This deadfall, if they are curious enough just to enter inside and put their foot on the trigger stick, they are yours if the trap is set properly.

CANADIAN TRIP FALL

This style of deadfall can be successfully, used over skunk holes, game runways and there you do away with the bait yard. This style of trap is much easier made, as it requires very little skill. Just a few straight sticks about the size round of a cane, a little twine. You can catch most any animal from a weasel to a raccoon. The illustration shows the "fall" or upper pole weighted. In our experience we have found it more satisfactory to have the "fall" heavy enough to kill the animal without the weight. It is often hard for the trapper to find a pole of the right size and weight for the "fall" and the next best way is to place additional weight as shown.

First make a pen in the form of a wigwam, driving stakes well into the ground to keep the animal away from the rear of the trap. It should be open on one side. Place a short log in front of the opening and at both ends of this drive stakes to hold it in place and for the long log to work up and down in. The top log should be six or eight feet long, according to size of animal you aim to use trap for, and about the same size as the bottom log. Cut a forked stick about 12 inches long for the bait stick, notching one end and tapering the other as shown in Fig. No. 2. A stick 24 inches long should then be cut and flattened at both ends.

FIG. 1   FIG. 2

THE TURN TRIGGER

To set the trap, raise one end of the upper log and stick one end of the flattened stick under it, resting it upon the top of the stake on the outside of the log. Place the bait stick, point downward, inside the pen upon a chip of wood or rock to keep it from sinking into the ground and set flat stick in the notch. When the animal pulls at the bait it turns the bait stake and throws the cross piece out of the notch of the bait stick and let the top log fall.

CHAPTER X

HOW TO SET

In explaining size pen some make them 2 feet long, writes a New York trapper, while one 12 inches long (as used on this trail), is sufficient; not only that, but it is superior for the following reasons: A 2 foot pen would let the animal pass inside and beyond the drop when sprung, unless the animal stepped on the treddle.

The Indians' trap is made by cutting a sapling 3 or 4 inches in diameter off the butt end cut a piece 2 foot and place on the ground for a bed piece; drive four stakes, two on either side of bed piece, leaving a space between of 12 inches, using the balance of pole for the drop to play between the stakes. For balance of pen a few stakes, bark or slabs cut from a tree.

For a spindle, cut from a hemlock, spruce or other dry limb a piece eight or ten inches long, sharpen one end to a point, the other end flatten a trifle for an inch or two on the underside, so that when placed on the bed piece it will lay steady. Now with a sharp knife, commence 1/2 inch back, and round off top side of spindle on which to place a standard four inches in length, cut from same material as spindle.

In setting, place the bait on the spindle so as to leave a space of only six inches from bait to the standard; now take spindle in left hand, standard in right hand, kneel down, raise the drop placing one knee under it to hold it up the right height. Lay spindle onto center of bed piece and place the standard on top of spindle, letting drop rest on top of standard so as to keep the pieces in position. Now by moving the standard out or in on the spindle, the spring of the trap can be so gauged that it will set safely for weeks or months, sprung easily, and hold anything from a weasel to a raccoon.

It is sure, as it kills immediately, giving them no chance to escape by twisting or gnawing off their legs. It is not so quickly made and set as a steel trap, and never gives "Sneakums" inducements to approach it for future use. After the trap is set, place bark or something suitable between the stakes above the drop and cover top of pen so as to compel the animal to enter in front, and at the same time ward off snow and sleet from interfering with its workings. Weight the drop pole on either side of pen by placing on chunks of wood or stone.

There are several ways to set deadfalls, as different triggers are used. The manner in constructing these traps is varied somewhat in the different sections. The illustration shown here is of a trap that is used to a considerable extent in all parts of America. The trapper for marten in the far North, the opossum trapper of West Virginia, Kentucky and Missouri, the skunk trapper of the New England States and the mink trapper of the west have all used this trap with success. It is for the hundreds of young and inexperienced trappers that the deadfall is shown here.

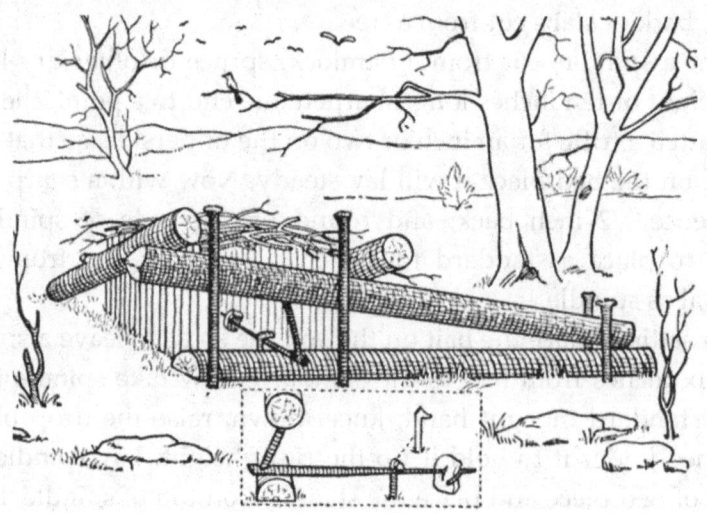

TWO PIECE TRIGGER TRAP

The trigger as shown, that is the one extending back into the pen, is all one piece. This trigger is usually cut from a bush and often requires some time to find one suited. If you intend to build a few traps of this kind it is well to be on the lookout in advance for suitable triggers. This trap is set with only two triggers, the one with the straight part extending back into the pen and the prong on which the "fall" is resting and the other trigger is driven into the ground so that it is only a little higher than the under log of the trap.

This trap can be set with the triggers known as figure 4 if preferred. Coon, mink, opossum, skunk and marten are usually not hard to catch in deadfalls, although now and then an animal for some reason is extremely hard to catch.

In building deadfalls it is best to split the end of the pole fartherest from the pen or bait and drive the stake there. This will hold the upper or "fall" pole solid, so that there will be no danger of its turning of its own weight and falling.

I enclose plan and description of a deadfall I have used with success on skunk and other fur animals, writes a trapper from New York State. Never having seen anything like it described I thought it might be a help to those using these traps. During November and December, 1897, I caught 11 skunk in one deadfall like this one.

STRING AND TRIGGER TRAP

Stakes are driven in the ground to form the pen same as on figure 4 or other deadfall, but no brush or sticks should be laid on top of pen as it would prevent the vertical stick from lifting up, A small log or board with stones on may be laid on pole for more weight. The pole may be from ten to fifteen feet long and about three inches in diameter. AA 18 inches or more out of the ground and one-half inch in diameter; B 20 inches, X one-half inch; C about 16 X 3/4 inches; D 20 X 3/4 inches; E same as AA only not crotch; F 1/4 inch. Rope long enough to go around pole and over B and tie around C. D should be from 1 to 3 inches above ground according to what is being trapped. Bait should be laid on ground or fastened to stake near middle of pen.

CHAPTER XI

WHEN TO BUILD

If you have determined upon your trapping ground it is best to build your traps in advance of the trapping season, so that they will become old and weather beaten. This, of course, is not necessary as traps are often built, baited and on the return of the trapper the following morning game securely caught. While the above is often true, deadfalls can and should be built in advance of the trapping season. There are at least two reasons for this: first, it allows the traps to become weather beaten and game is not so suspicious; second, all the trapper has to do when the trapping season arrives is to visit and set his traps.

Some object to deadfalls on the ground that they require lots of work to build and that a trapper's time is valuable at this season of the year. Such may be true of the amateur, but the professional trapper usually has much idle time in August, September and early October, when he is glad to look out for trapping grounds for the coming winter. It is a day's work for one man to build from eight to twelve deadfalls, depending of course upon how convenient he finds the pole to make the fall. The other material is usually not hard to find or make. That is stakes, chunks and rocks. If you only build six or eight traps and construct them right they are worth twice as many poorly built. When properly built they will last for years, requiring but little mending each fall at the opening of the trapping season. Taken all in all we do not know that a certain number of deadfalls take up any more time than an equal number of steel traps. In fact more deadfalls can be set in a day, after they are built, than steel traps.

When it is stated that you will perhaps do as well at home as elsewhere, this, of course, depends upon where you are located, how many trappers there are in your section, etc. If there is but little to be caught then you had best go elsewhere, but trappers have been known in thickly settled sections to catch from $50 to $300 worth of fur in a season, lasting from November 1 to March 15. Of course in the far north, where trapping can be carried on from October 15 to June 15, or eight months, the catch is much larger, and as the animals caught are more valuable, the catch of a single trapper is sometimes as high as $600 to $1,000.

The trapper who stays near home has the advantage of knowing the territory. If he was to visit a strange section, altho a good trapping locality, he would not do so well as if he were acquainted with the locality and knew the locations of the best dens. Then again his expenses are heavier if he goes into a strange section, yet If there is but little game near your home, and you are going to make a business of trapping, go and look up a good trapping section. Under these conditions it is best for two or three to go together. There is no necessity of carrying but little baggage other than your gun, for at the season of the year that prospecting is done there is but little difficulty in killing enough game to live on.

After you have once found a good trapping section, and built your cabin, deadfalls and snares, you can go there fall after fall with your line of steel traps, resetting your deadfalls with but little repairs for years. You will also become better acquainted with the territory each season and will make larger catches. Do not think that you have caught all the game the first season, for generally upon your return the next fall you will find signs of game as numerous as ever.

In locating new trapping grounds, if two or three are together and it is a busy time in September, let one of the party go in advance prospecting. This will save much valuable time when you make the start for the fall and winter trapping campaign. It will pay you to know where you are going before you make the final start.

CHAPTER XII

WHERE TO BUILD

In determining where to set deadfalls or locate snares if you will keep in mind the dens where each winter you have caught fur-bearing animals, or their tracks have often been seen in the snow or mud, and build your traps and construct snares at or near such places you are pretty sure to not go astray.

The location, of course, depends largely upon what kind of game you are trying to catch. If mink or coon, there is no better place than along streams where there are dens. If there should be a small branch leading off from the main stream, at the mouth of this is often an excellent place to locate a trap. It should not be too near the water as a rise would damage or perhaps float off at least part of your trap. Sometimes farther up this small stream there are bluffs and rocks; at such places, if there are dens, is just the place to build deadfalls. If there are several dens, and the bluff extends along several hundred feet, it perhaps will pay to build two or three traps here.

In cleared fields, woods or thickets skunk are found anywhere that there are dens you can construct a trap. While, as a rule, the thinly settled districts are the best trapping sections, yet skunk, muskrat and red fox are found in greatest numbers in settled sections, while opossum, raccoon and mink are found in fairly well settled districts. It is therefore not necessary that you should go to the wilderness to make fairly good catches. While the trapper in the wilderness has the advantage of no one disturbing his deadfalls, yet he has disadvantages. The trapper who means business need not go hundreds of miles away, but if he will build a line of traps along some stream where there are mink, or in the thickets and along rocky buffs for skunk, raccoon, opossum, etc., he will be surprised at results.

In some sections land owners may not allow trapping, but

usually they will, especially if you take the pains to ask before you commence building or setting your traps.

The fact that you have your traps scattered over a large territory gives you better chances of making good catches, for most animals travel quite a distance from night to night. You may have traps at some stream that is eight or ten miles from your home and a mink may come along that does most of its seeking for food miles farther up or down this stream, nearer, perhaps, where it was raised, and you get him. Thus you see by going only ten miles away you may catch animals that really live twenty. Just how far a mink may travel up or down a creek or river I do not know, but it is certain that they go many miles and traps may make a catch of a mink that lives many, many miles away. Of course along small streams they may not go so far. Often, however, they continue their travels from one stream to another.

If you are an expert trapper you can very easily detect, if you are in a good locality, especially if in the fall — September and October. These are the two months when the most prospecting is done. Going along streams at this season tracks are plainly seen and in the forests at dens signs, such as hair, bones and dung. Often you will come upon signs where some bird has been devoured and you know that some animal has been in the locality. Old trappers readily detect all these signs and new ones can learn by experience.

It is not absolutely necessary to build traps at or near dens. Some years ago, I remember when doing considerable trapping in Southern Ohio, I came upon a deadfall built near a small stream that ran thru a woods. I looked around for dens, but saw none. Why this trap had been built there was a puzzle to me. One day I happened upon the owner of the trap and asked him what he expected to catch in that trap.

In reply he pointed to a bush some rods distant in which hung the carcasses of two opossum and one coon — caught in the trap. While there were no dens near, it was a favorite place for animals to cross or else they came there for water. This same trap was the means of this old trapper taking two or three animals each winter, while other traps at dens near caught less. There is much in knowing where to set traps, but keep your eyes open for signs and you will learn where to build traps and set snares sooner or later.

Yes, boys, the deadfall is a splendid trap if made right, says an Arkansas trapper. I will tell you how to make one that will catch every mink and coon that runs the creek. Take a pole four feet long and four inches through, next get a log six inches through and eight feet long. Use eight stakes and two switches. Use the figure four trigger, but the notches are cut different. Both of the notches are cut on the top side of the long trigger and a notch cut in the upright trigger and down the long trigger. The paddle part is sixteen inches long. When the trap is set the paddle wants to be level and one-half inch higher than small logs, then your two switches comes in this to keep the paddle from hitting the bark on side logs.

TRAIL OR DEN TRAP

Next is where to set. If along a creek, find a place where the water is within three feet of the bank, set your trap up and down the creek at edge of water, dam up from back end of paddle to bank with brush or briars, then from front end into water three or four feet. You will find the upright trigger has to be a good deal longer than the notch trigger. You can use round triggers if you want to by nailing a shingle five inches wide on the long trigger stick. Be sure

59

and have your paddle muddy if setting along creeks. You want to put a little stone back beyond paddle, so when the trap falls it will not burst paddle. Now you have a trap easy made and sure to catch any animal that steps on paddle, which is five inches wide and sixteen long. You don't need any bait, but you can use bait by throwing it under paddle. This trap is hard to beat for small game.

I make a deadfall that sets without bait, writes an Illinois trapper. It is made like any other only different triggers. Set it across path, over or in front of den or remove a rail and set it in the corner of a fence where game goes thru. Use thread in dry weather, fine wire for wet. Two logs for bottom is better than one, make triggers high enough to suit the animal you wish to catch; if he hits the string or wire he is yours.

CHAPTER XIII

THE PROPER BAIT

Bait is sometimes difficult to get, but usually the trapper will get enough with his gun and steel traps to keep his line of deadfalls well baited, without difficulty. In trapping, all animals caught after the pelt is taken off should be hung up so that other animals cannot reach them, but will visit your traps.

There are two objects in hanging up bait: First, other animals coming along are apt to eat them and not visit your deadfall; second, should you run out of bait you can cut a piece from the animal hanging up, bait your trap and go to the next. While bait of this kind is not recommended, sometimes it comes to this or nothing. Fresh bait is what is wanted at all times, yet the trapper cannot always get what he knows is best and consequently must do the next best. Perhaps by his next visit he has bait in abundance.

The writer has known trappers to use a piece of skunk, opossum, muskrat, coon, etc., that had been caught some weeks before and hung up in a sapling where it froze and on the next visit the trap baited with skunk contained a skunk. This shows that when an animal is very hungry it is not very particular what it eats.

In the early fall while food of all kinds is easy to find, any animal is harder to entice to bait and at this season bait should be fresh if the trapper expects to make profitable catches. The trapper should always carry a gun, pistol or good revolver with which to help kill game to supply bait for his traps. Steel traps set along the line will also help to keep the supply of bait up at all times. If you are successful in securing a great deal of bait, more than will be used on that round, you will find it an excellent idea to leave some at certain places where it can be secured on the next round should it be needed.

Bait may consist of any tough bit of meat, but rabbit is an excellent bait. Quail or almost any bird is good. Chicken also makes good bait. Squirrel is all right. For mink, fish is excellent. Mice, frogs and muskrat can all be used. Remember that the fresher and bloodier the bait the better — animals will scent it much quicker. They are also fonder of fresh bait than that which has been killed for days or weeks as the case may be.

In baiting it is important to see that the bait is on secure. It is a good idea to tie it on with strong thread or small cord. The amount of bait to put on a single trap is not so important. Most trappers use a rabbit in baiting ten traps or less; the head makes bait for one trap, each foreleg another, the back about three and each hind leg one, altho each hind leg can be cut to make bait for two traps.

The spindle or trigger is run thru the bait and should be fastened on trigger near the end as shown in illustration elsewhere. The securing of bait on the trigger is an important thing. If it is not on securely and the trap is hard to get off, the animal may devour bait and the trap not fall. If the trigger is only sticking loosely in the bait, it is easy for an animal to steal the bait. Usually the observing trapper knows these things and are on their guard, but for those who are using deadfalls this season for the first time, more explicit explanation is necessary.

The bait should extend back into the pen about a foot and the pen should be so constructed that the bait touches nowhere only on the trigger. The animal in eating the bait usually stands with its fore feet upon the under pole, or just over it. In this condition it can readily be seen, that if its gnawing at the bait twists the trigger off the upright prop what the consequences will be — the animal will be caught across the back. An animal standing in the position just described will naturally pull down somewhat on the bait and in its eagerness to get the bait pulls and twists the spindle, or trigger, off the upright prop.

It is a good idea to try the trigger. That is, place the triggers under the fall just the same as you would if they were baited and you were going to set the trap. By doing this you will find out about how you want to set the triggers so that they will work properly. There is much in being acquainted with the working of traps. Study them carefully and you will soon learn to be a successful trapper.

62

CHAPTER XIV

TRAPS KNOCKED OFF

If you find that your traps are "down" each time you visit them and the bait gone, the pen is perhaps too large and the animal, if a small one like a mink, is going inside to devour bait. Animals usually stand with fore feet upon lower log and reach into pen after bait, but at times they have been known to go inside. In this case the animal is not in danger as when the "fall" comes down the animal is not under it. If such is the case, that is, the animal entirely inside the pen, the trigger will be caught under the fall and the trapper knows that whatever is molesting his trap is doing so from the inside. All that the trapper has to do is lessen the size of the pen. This can be done by placing small stones or chunks on the inside of the pen or by driving stakes on the inside. By doing this the outside appearance is not changed.

If, on the other hand, the trigger, that is the long one or spindle, not the short prop, is pulled out each time and often carried several feet, the trap is set too hard to "fall" and should be set easier. If the prop, or upright piece, is cut square across the top, take your knife and round off the edges so that the trigger will slip off easier. Again the pen may be torn down and the animal takes bait from the rear. Here is where it pays to build traps substantial. In such cases rebuild the pen, making it stronger. Should it be torn down on subsequent visits, the game is perhaps a fox. Of course if the pen has been torn down by some trapper or passing hunter, you can readily detect same by the manner in which it has been done. If the trapper is satisfied that it is an animal that is doing the mischief, he wants to plan carefully, and if he is an expert trapper, a steel trap or two will come into good play and the animal will be caught in the steel trap. The pen will not be torn down again.

When traps are down note carefully the condition that they are in; see that the "fall" fits on the lower pole closely, and by the way, when building this is an important thing to notice — that the fall fits snugly on the lower or under pole.

If a snare or spring pole is up but nothing caught, simply reset. Should many snares be up "thrown" and no catches, the trouble should be located at once. The noose is probably too large or small or made of limber or too stiff string or wire, or maybe it is too securely fastened. When resetting, note all these carefully and experience will sooner or later enable you to set just right to make a catch. If a certain snare is bothered continually, it will do no harm to set a steel trap where you think chances best of taking the animal. It matters but little to the trapper how the animal is caught, as it is his pelt that is wanted.

In using the trip triggers with or without bait, the trapper should fasten the bait by either driving a peg through it and into the ground or tieing.

In most instances the animal will throw the trap before getting to the bait, but it is well to take this precaution in case, for any reason, the animal should not step on the trip trigger at first.

Sometimes a small animal may jump over the trip trigger in order to get the bait and in its endeavor to get bait will strike the trigger. The animal does not know that the trigger is dangerous, but now and then either steps or jumps over. Generally they step on the trigger, for if the trapper is "onto his job" the bait and trigger are so placed that the animal thinks the trip trigger is the place to put his foot.

In using without bait the trigger is so arranged that the animal rubs or steps on the trigger when entering or leaving the pen or if at a trail or runway when passing along.

CHAPTER XV

SPRING POLE SNARE

While the deadfall is good for most animals, there is no one trap that fills all requirements and in all places. Some animals may be shy of deadfalls that can be taken in spring poles, snares and steel traps. This trap is easily and cheaply constructed. It should be made near dens or where animals travel frequently.

If a small bush is not growing handy, cut one. Drive a stake deeply in the ground, pull it out, stick the larger end of the bush cut into it. The explanation of this trap is as follows: 1, bait stick; 2, trigger; 3, noose made of wire or stout cord; 4, stay wire made of wire or cord; 5, bait; 6, spring pole.

By noting carefully the illustration this trap can be built easily. The size of the bush or spring pole, of course, depends upon what sized animals you are trapping. This trap will take small game such as mink, opossum, skunk, etc., or can be made large and strong enough to catch mountain lion or black bear.

SPRING POLE AND SNARE

The snare is made by building a round fence in a place where there is plenty of small trees. Select two about four inches apart for noose and snare entrance, and another long springy one for spring pole 6 or 7 feet long, bend this down and trim it. Have a noose made of limber wire or strong string and a cross piece. Having cut notches in the sides of the trees for the same to fit, have it to spring easy. For snaring rabbits have the fence quite high.

SMALL GAME SNARE

Observe the above description and you can readily make. No. 1 is the noose, No. 2 is spring pole, No. 3 fence, No. 4 bait. This snare already explained can be made any time in the year while the dead fall can only be constructed when the ground isn't frozen.

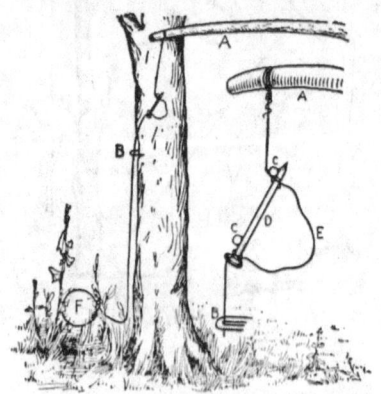

WIRE AND TWINE SNARE

The snares can be either made of twine or wire. Many fox and lynx snare trappers in the North use small brass wire.

Snares work well in cold weather and if properly constructed are pretty sure catchers.

A — Spring pole.

B — Staple.

C — Two small nails driven in tree. (Three inch nail head, end down, with snare looped at each end with a foot of slack between. As soon as the D — three inch nail is pulled down, it will slip past the nail at top end, when spring pole will instantly take up the slack, also the fox, to staple and does its work.)

E — Slack line or wire.

F — Loop should be 7 inches in diameter and bottom of loop ten inches from the ground.

Remarks — The nails should be driven above staple so it will pull straight down to release the snare fastening.

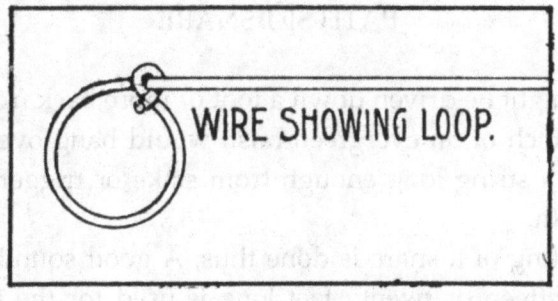

WIRE SHOWING LOOP.

SNARE LOOP

A great many foxes have been caught in this country by the plan of the drawing outlined, writes J. C. Hunter, of Canada. A — the snare, should be made of rabbit wire, four or five strand twisted together. Should be long enough to make a loop about seven inches in diameter when set. Bottom side of snare should be about six inches from the ground. E — is a little stick, sharp at one end and split at the other, to stick in the ground and slip bottom of snare in split end, to hold snare steady.

B — is catch to hold down spring pole. C — is stake. D — is spring pole. Some bend down a sapling for a spring pole, but we think the best way is to cut and trim up a small pole about ten feet long; fasten the big end under a root and bend it down over a crotch, stake or small tree. Snare should be set on a summer sheep path, where it goes through the bushes.

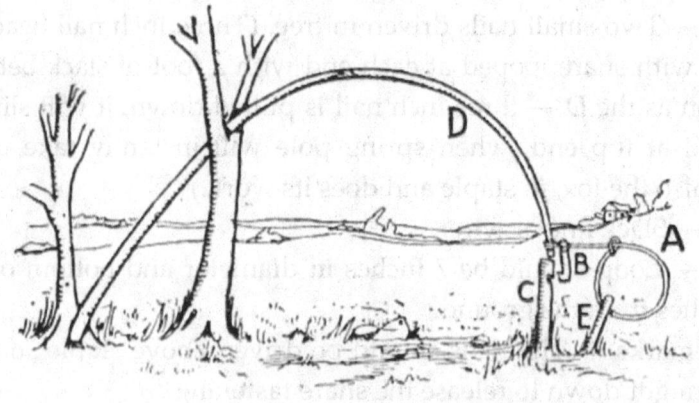

PATH SET SNARE

Stake might be driven down a foot or more back from the path, where a branch of an evergreen bush would hang over it so as to hide it and a string long enough from stake or trigger to snare to rest over path.

The setting of a snare is done thus: A good sound tamarac or other pole fifteen or twenty feet long is used for the tossing. The butt end of this must be five or six inches in diameter and the small end about three inches. A tree with a crotch in it is then selected to balance the pole upon. Failing to find such a tree in the proper place, an artificial fork is made by crossing two stout young birch or tamarac, firmly planted in the ground, and the two upper points tied together six or ten inches from the top. The balancing or tossing pole is lodged in this fork so that the part towards the butt would out-weigh a bear of two or three hundred pounds suspended from the small end.

Next a stout little birch or spruce is selected and a section of three or four cut off. From this all the branches are removed, except one, the small end is pointed and driven deep into the ground a few inches at one side of the bear road. The snare is made of three twisted strands of eighteen thread cod line and is firmly tied to the tossing pole. A few dried branches are stuck in the ground each side of the path, the pole is depressed so the very end is caught under the twig on the stick driven in the ground for that purpose and the noose is stiffened by rubbing balsam branches which leave enough gum to make it hold its shape.

The noose is kept in the proper position (the bottom being about sixteen inches above the road and the diameter being about eleven inches) by blades of dry grass looped to it and the ends let into a gash on sticks at each side, put there for that purpose. No green branches are used in the hedge about the road because this would make the bear suspicious. The snare is now complete and the hunter stands back and examines it critically. His last act is to rub some beaver castor on the trunk of some tree standing near the road, ten or twelve feet from the snare. This is done on another tree at the same distance on the opposite side of the snare.

Bears are attracted by the smell of the castor and rub themselves against the tree in the same way as a dog rubs on carrion. When finished rubbing on one tree he scents the other and in going to get at the fresh one tries to pass thru the snare. He feels the noose tighten about his neck and struggles; this pulls the end of the tossing pole from under the branch trigger, up goes the pole and old Bruin with it.

My way, according to a Massachusetts trapper, to trap skunk without scenting, and it is successful, is to snare them. Use a spring pole and if one does not grow handy, cut one and set it up as firmly as possible about four or five feet from the burrow and to one side. Probably the ground is frozen and you will have to brace it up with logs or stones or perhaps lash it to a stump or root. When the top of the pole is bent down it should be caught under the end of a log or rock on the opposite side of the hole so that it can easily be dislodged by an animal, either going in or out of the burrow.

The snare or noose is attached to the spring pole directly over the center of the burrows and the bottom of the noose should be an inch and a half or two inches from the ground to allow the animal's feet to pass under it and his little pointed nose to go thru the center. Set the noose as closely over the entrance of the hole as possible and one or two carefully arranged twigs will keep it in place.

Strong twine is better for the noose than large cord as the skunk is less liable to notice it. When a skunk passes in or out of the hole the noose becomes tightened about his neck and a slight pull releases the spring pole which soon strangles him. While this may seem an elaborate description of so simple a trap, still, like any other trap, if set in a careless, half-hearted manner, it will meet with indifferent success and, tho simple the snare, with a little thought and ingenuity can be applied in almost any situation for the capture of small game.

CHAPTER XVI

TRAIL SET SNARE

Many of the boys, writes an Indiana trapper, have come forth with their particular snares and methods of making same, all of which I believe are good, but most of them require to be baited, which is one bad feature as applied to certain districts, for such has been my experience that in many localities it is utterly impossible to get animals to take bait. This snare may be used as a blind or set with bait as your trapping grounds, or rather the animals, may require.

It is very inexpensive and so simple any boy can make it. First get a strip of iron one-eighth inch thick, three-eighths or one-half wide. Cut it in nine inch lengths and bend in the shape of Fig. 2, having drilled a one-fourth inch hole in either end. Next secure some light sheet iron, or heavy tin, cut in pieces 2 3/4 inches by 5 3/4 inches for the pan, and drill a one-fourth inch hole in center of same as shown in Fig. 3. It is now a very easy matter to rivet the pan or Fig. 3 to Fig. 2. This done, take some 20 penny spikes and cut off the heads as per Fig. 1.

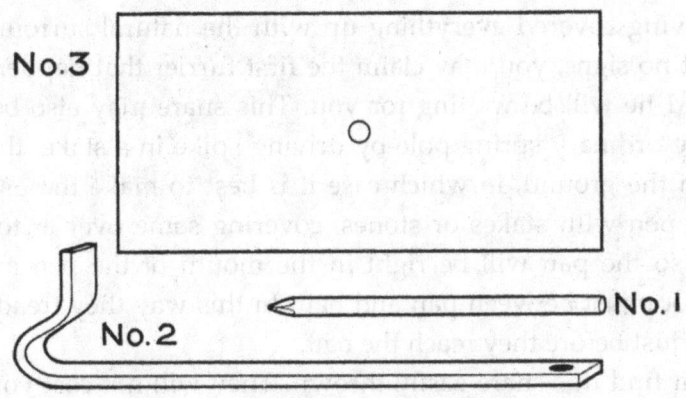

No.3

No.2

No. I

TRIP PAN OR PLATE

Now brass, or preferably copper wire, can be had on spools at most any hardware store, which is used for the loops, as it is so pliable yet sufficiently strong to hold any of the small fur bearers, as it is made in many sizes. Use the brass or copper wire only for the loops, as ordinary stove pipe wire is just the article for the finishing of the snare.

For a blind set to be placed in the run of the animals, make a double loop, that is, two loops for each snare. Now, take a bunch of these with you and find the runs or follow the ravines and creeks where they feed. If you can find a tree in a favorable spot on their runs, take one of your headless spikes and drive in the base of the tree a few inches from the ground.

Now take No. 2 with the pan riveted thereon and hook bent and over spike, driving spike into tree until pan is level and until there is just room enough to hook loop of wire over head of spike. (See illustration.) Dig out under pan so same can fall when stepped upon. Then secure a rock or chunk of sufficient weight and fasten to other end of wire. Throw this over limb of tree and hook loop over head of a spike, having first put No. 2 in place.

Put one loop on one side of the pan and the other loop on the other side, so that an animal coming either way will step upon the pan to his sorrow. This done, drive a staple in tree over wire running from spike to limb, which will prevent the animal being pulled over the limb and escaping.

Having covered everything up with the natural surroundings and left no signs, you may claim the first furrier that happens that way and he will be waiting for you. This snare may also be used with the ordinary spring pole by driving spike in a stake, then the stake in the ground, in which case it is best to make the usual V-shaped pen with stakes or stones, covering same over at top and setting so the pan will be right in the mouth of the pen and the single loop just between pan and bait. In this way they tread upon the pan just before they reach the bait.

You find this snare easily thrown. They will not cost you over three cents a piece, and any man can easily carry one hundred of them and not be half loaded.

DOUBLE TRAIL SET

In many ways the snare is splendid for lynx. Here in Western Ontario, says a well known trapper, where the lynx seldom take bait, they may be taken quite easily in snares set on snowshoe trails. Fig. 1 shows a wire snare set on such a trail. I go about it in the following manner: Having found a suitable place along the edge of some swamp or alder thicket, I cut a spruce or balsam tree, about ten or twelve feet long, and throw it across the trail. I press the tree down until the stem of the tree is about twenty inches above the trail, and make an opening in the trail by cutting a few of the limbs away on the under side of the trail. Then I set a couple of dead stakes on each side so as to leave the opening about ten inches wide and hang my snare between these stakes and directly under the stem of the tree.

73

The snare should be about nine inches in diameter and should be fastened securely to the tree. It should also be fastened lightly to the stakes on either side, so it will not spring out of shape. The best way is to make a little split in the side of each stake, and fasten the snare with a very small twig stuck in the split stake.

I make the snares of rabbit wire, about four or five plies thick, twisted. Some trappers prefer to use a cord. The dark colored codfish line is best, and it is best to use a spring pole snare, and Fig. 3 shows the method of tieing and fastening to the stakes. It will be seen that when the lynx passes his head through the snare he only needs to give a slight pull to open the slip knot and release the spring pole.

To prevent the rabbits from biting a cord snare, rub it well with the dropping of the lynx or fox and also, never use any green wood other than spruce or balsam, as any fresh green wood is sure to attract the rabbits. You may also put a small piece of beaver castor along the trail on each side of the snare, and you will be more sure of the lynx, as beaver castor is very attractive to these big cats.

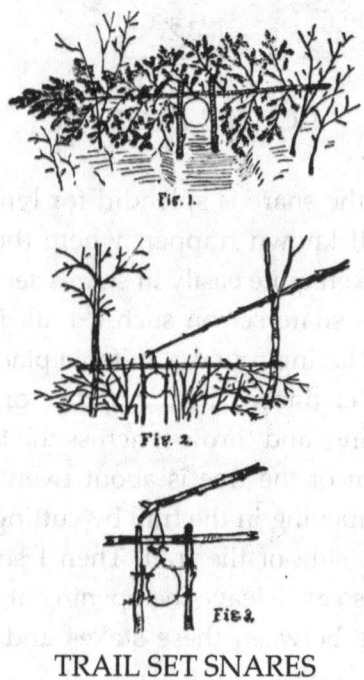

Fig. 1.

Fig. 2.

Fig 3.

TRAIL SET SNARES

74

We will now proceed to make another spring pole snare, altho the one described before is more practical, says a Colorado trapper. It is made like the preceding one except the trigger, etc. This one is to be used on a runway without any bait whatever. The illustration shows the trigger as it appears in the runway. No. 1 is the trip stick; No. 2, the stay crotch; No. 3, the trigger; No. 4, the loop; No. 5, the pathway, and No. G, the stay wire.

PATH SNARE

The animal in coming on down the path (5) passes its body or neck thru the loop made of stout soft insulated wire (4); in passing it steps on the trip stick (1) which settles with the animal's weight, releasing the trigger (3) which in turn releases the stay wire (6) and jerks the loop (4) around the animal; the spring pole onto which the stay-wire it attached lifts your game up into the air, choking it to death and placing it out of reach of other animals that would otherwise destroy your fur. A small notch cut in the stay crotch where the end of the trip stick rests will insure the trigger to be released. This will hold the trip stick firm at the end, making it move only at the end where the animal steps.

CHAPTER XVII

BAIT SET SNARE

This snare I consider good for such animals as will take bait.

No. 1 and 2, headless wire nails driven horizontally into tree about ten inches from ground.

No. 3, a No. 10 or 12 wire nail with head used to catch under No. 1 and 2.

No. 4, bait stick or trigger. No. 3 passes through No. 4.

No. 5, bait, frog tied to bottom of No. 4.

No. 6's snare, fastened to No. 3 by two half hitches, then fastened to No. 3 by two half hitches, then fastened to seven or spring pole.

No. 7, spring pole.

Nos. 8, 8, small stakes driven in ground to form a pen.

Nos. 9, 9, two small twigs split at top to hold snare loop in place.

Nos. 1 and 2 should be about 4 inches apart.

No. 3 goes through a gimlet hole in No. 4. About three inches from the top use any small round stick from 1/2 to 1 inch in thickness, not necessary to flatten No. 4 as in illustration. Use it natural bark on. From hole in No. 4 to bottom end should be about 7 inches.

Snare loop about 6 inches in front of bait, held in place by 9, 9, slightly leaning against 8,8.

It can be plainly seen that if an animal takes No. 5 in its jaws and tries to remove it, it moves out the bottom of No. 4, moving forward No. 3 until, flip! up she goes. The top of No. 4 must be tight against the tree when set.

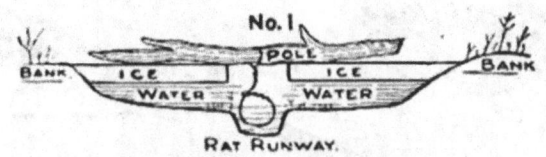

RAT RUNWAY SNARE.

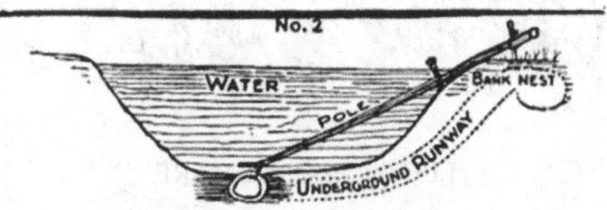

UNDERGROUND RAT RUNWAY.

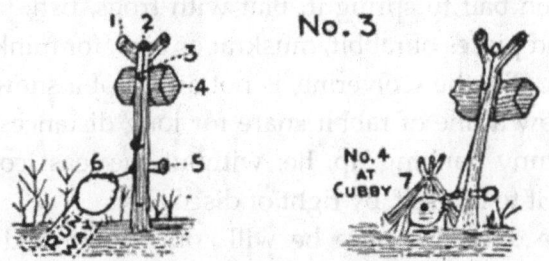

RUNWAY AND CUBBY SET.

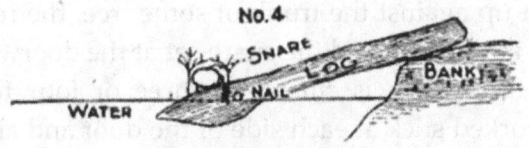

LOG SET SNARE.

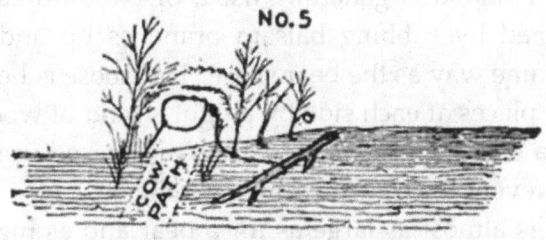

COW PATH SNARE.

77

LIFTING POLE SNARE

No. 3 should just catch under No. 1 and 2, then it takes but 1/2 inch to pull on bait to spring it. Bait with frogs, fish, tainted meat for skunk, and pieces of rabbit, muskrat or bird, for mink.

The lynx, like the wolverine, is not afraid of a snowshoe track, and will follow a line of rabbit snare for long distances, and when he sees a bunny hanging up, he, without the least compunction, appropriates it to himself, by right of discovery.

When he does this once he will come again and the Indian hunter, knowing this, at once sets a snare for "Mister Cat." Sometimes when the thief has left a portion of the rabbit, a branch house is built up against the trunk of some tree, the remains of the rabbit placed at the back and the snare set at the doorway.

A stout birch stick is cut about three or four feet long and lodged on a forked stick at each side of the door and about two and a half feet high. To the middle of this crossbar the end of the twine is tied; No. 9 Holland is generally used, or No. 6 thread cod line. This is gummed by rubbing balsam branches up and down the twine in the same way as the bear snare. The noose is held in shape in one or two places at each side by a light strand of wood or blade of grass and a couple of small dry sticks are placed upright under the snare to prevent the cat from passing beneath.

The loop is almost as large as for a bear and as high from the ground, if not higher. The lynx has long legs and carries his head straight in front of him and takes a snare by pushing thru it, or by a rush, never crouching and then springing.

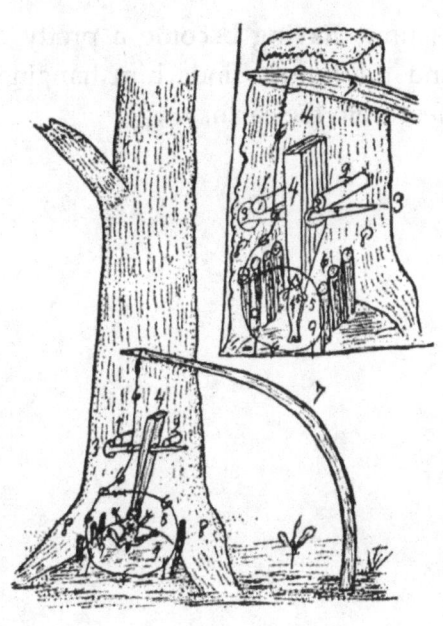

BAIT SET SNARE

As the resort of rabbits is a young growth of country, there are also lynx in the greatest numbers. Rabbits and partridges are their principal food. When the Indian enters a new piece of country to set rabbit snares to support his wife and family and sees signs of lynx, he combines the two kinds of hunting and as he goes along, once in a while, he bars his snowshoe track by placing a lynx snare in the way. The lynx are fond of the smell of castor, as indeed are most animals, so the hunter rubs a little on a tree at each side of his snare for the cat to rub against when he comes that way.

The snare is never tied to anything immovable, as they are very powerful and would break the twine. As soon as the noose tightens the cross piece comes readily away from the supports and the cat springs to one side. The stick, however, either knocks him a blow or gets tangled in his legs. This he tries several times, but with the same result, that bothersome stick is always hanging to his neck. About the last effort he makes to free himself is to ascend a tree. This, however, is nearly always fatal, for after he gets up a certain distance this trouble some stick is sure to get fast back of some limb.

The lynx by this time, having become a pretty cross cat, makes matters worse and the hunter finds him hanging dead, at times twenty or thirty feet from the earth.

CHAPTER XVIII

THE BOX TRAP

This trap is put to various uses. The beginner usually has one or two with which he traps for rabbits. In fact they are great for that for the animal is not injured, which is often the case when shot or caught by dogs. Rabbits caught in box traps are therefore the best for eating.

The trapper who wants to secure fur-bearers alive to sell to parks, menageries or to start a "fur ranch" usually uses the box trap.

The size for rabbits is about 30 inches long by 5 wide and 6 high. The boards can be of any kind but pine, poplar, etc., being light is much used. The boards need only be a half inch thick. To make a trap you will need four pieces 30 inches long; two of these for the sides should be six inches wide; the other two for top and bottom should be 5 inches. These pieces should be nailed on the top and bottom of the sides. This will make the inside of the trap six inches high by four wide. It is best to have your trap narrow so that the animal you are trapping cannot turn in the trap.

In one end of the trap wires or small iron rods should be placed (see illustration). These should be about an inch apart. In the other end the door is constructed. This can be made out of wire also. The bottom of door should strike about eight inches inside. It will be seen that an animal pushing against the door, from the outside, raises it, but once on the inside the more they push against it the tighter it becomes.

The trap can be set at holes where game is known to be, or can be placed where game frequents and baited. If bait is used place a little prop under the door and place bait back in trap a foot or more. Bait to use of course depending upon what you are trapping.

The trap described is about right size for the common rabbit and mink. For skunk and opossum a trap a little larger will be required.

For mink and other animals that are gnawers the traps should be visited daily for they may gnaw and escape. If impossible to visit traps daily they should be lined with tin.

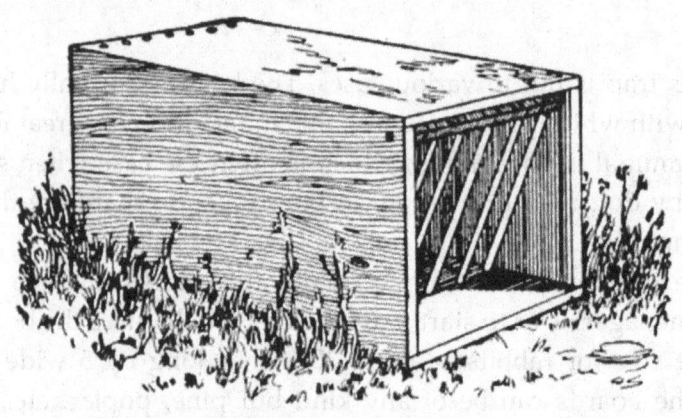

THE BOX TRAP

In many places these traps, with a door at each end, are used for catching muskrat. They are set in their dens under water and either tied or weighted down. The rats are caught either going in or leaving.

In making these traps the beginner is apt to make them too wide — so the animal can turn within. This is a mistake for it gives the game more freedom and room to gnaw to liberty.

The animal simply goes in and is there until the trapper comes along and removes the game. Skunk can be drowned when caught in this trap without scenting if the trapper knows how to go about it.

The trap should be handled carefully. Take to water sufficiently deep to cover the trap and slowly sink and then either weight the trap or hold down until the animal is drowned.

The box trap is a humane trap if visited daily. They are rather unhandy to carry about and few trappers want many, yet under certain conditions they are very useful. They can be made during idle time. For mink and other shy animals they should be handled as little as possible. They should be made of old boards or at least avoid all appearances of newness.

Some sections saplings to make deadfalls cannot be had and for the benefit of such, a wooden trap, three feet long and six inches wide and deep, is a good manner to take muskrat, writes a Western trapper. The boards can be cut out of any old lumber. In each end is a wire door, hung on hinges at the top. These doors rise at the slightest push on the outside, but will not open from the inside. The trap is sunk in the water at the entrance to the den and is fastened there. A muskrat in entering or leaving the den is sure to enter the trap.

The animal, of course, could gnaw out, but will drown before it has time to accomplish this. Several rats are often taken, where they are numerous, in a night. Traps of this kind can be used to best advantage in lakes and ponds or where the height of the stream does not vary much. If they are set along creeks and rivers you want to fasten them securely or take them up before heavy rains, as they are almost sure to be washed away.

I see in a recent number where George Walker wanted some one to tell through H-T-T how to make box trap to catch muskrat. Here is a good way:

First take four boards 36 inches long, nail together leaving both ends open. Next a small gate, consisting of a square piece of wood supplied with a few stiff wires is then pivoted inside of each opening so as to work freely and fall easily when raised. The bait is fastened inside the center of the box. The animal in quest of the bait finds an easy entrance, as the wires lift at slight pressure, but the exit after the gate has closed is so difficult that escape is almost beyond question. To insure further strength it is advisable to connect the lower ends of the wires by a cross piece of fine wire twisted about each. If you have good luck you can catch two and three in this trap each night. Set in two or three inches of water where muskrat frequents, or set in skunk dens.

CHAPTER XIX

THE COOP TRAP

This trap is used with great success for catching wild turkey, pheasants, quail and other feathered game. In some states the law forbids the use of this and similar traps.

The trap is built like an ordinary rail pen. In fact, some use small rails when constructing this trap for wild turkey, while others build of small straight poles. The pen is usually six feet or more square and about three high. The "coop" is stronger if drawn in from bottom to top (see illustration). The top must be covered and weighted.

A ditch is now dug about a foot wide. This ditch should begin about three feet from coop and lead within. Corn or other grain is scattered on the outside and in the trench leading into the coop. On the inside considerable should be scattered in the leaves and small but short twigs.

The turkeys once on the inside will eat the grain and scratch among the leaves which generally partly fill the trench and as the birds are usually looking up, when not eating, they do not think of the trench thru which they entered.

The same trap will catch quail, but of course is built much smaller. About three feet square being large enough and a foot high is sufficient. Some have built quail coops out of cornstalks and report catches.

The quail coop should have the ditch leading to the inside the same as described for turkey. Of course the ditch should be much smaller — only large enough for one bird to enter at a time. On the inside of coop it is a good idea to lay a board six inches or wider over the ditch. The bait should be wheat or other small grain or seeds that the birds like. Scatter thinly on the outside and in the trench, but on the inside place more liberally. Chaff or leaves should be placed on the inside so that the birds in scratching for the grain will partly fill up the hole thru which they came.

THE COOP TRAP

Quail, turkey and other feathered game once on the inside and after eating the bait never think of going down into the ditch and out, but walk round and round the coop looking thru the chinks and trying to escape.

The largest catches are made by baiting where the birds frequent for some days or even weeks before trying to make a catch. It is well to make the coops long in advance so that the birds will be accustomed to them, especially wild turkey.

These traps are some times used with the figure 4 trigger, but when thus set seldom more than one or two birds are caught at a time.

CHAPTER XX

THE PIT TRAP

This method of catching game and fur bearing animals is not much used, as the labor in connection with making a pit trap is considerable. The method, however, is an excellent one for taking some of the larger animals, especially when they are wanted for parks, menageries, etc., uninjured.

The pit should be several feet deep and bait placed as shown. Another way is to cover the top with rotten limbs, leaves, etc., and place the bait on this. The animal in trying to secure the bait breaks thru.

The dirt from the pit should be removed in baskets. Catches are made by digging a pit across animal runways or trails. When the ground is not frozen or during rainy weather it is well to place a board several inches wide at top. The animal in going over its usual trail steps upon the frail covering and falls thru.

While the pit trap is mostly used for capturing large game, it can be used to advantage for taking many of the smaller fur bearers.

Where muskrat are numerous, instead of digging a pit, secure a box about three feet deep. The width and length make no difference. Place a few flat rocks in the bottom and place in the water where rats frequent. Make the box solid. The box must be water tight. The weight should bring the top of box to within a few inches of water. A couple of boards or chunks should be so placed that the rats will climb up them and to the box along the edge of which the bait is placed.

The pit trap can be used where skunk and other animals frequent. Bait the place for some days before the pit is dug.

If the pit is to be used without bait, then find the runways of the animal and dig the pit. While some animals may not be shy, if a little fresh dirt is lying around, yet it is best to be very careful and carry all earth taken out of pit a few rods to one side. Pits of this kind should be several feet deep.

THE PIT TRAP

The success the hunter or trapper has in using this method will depend largely upon his knowledge of the game he is after. Unless the animal or animals are wanted alive, the work to make a pit is too great and the chances of a catch never certain. This way is not practicable under ordinary circumstances, yet where the game is wanted alive and sound, is worth trying.

CHAPTER XXI

NUMBER OF TRAPS

In some localities there are not many dens and trappers make use of about all when trapping that section, but in other parts of the country dens are so numerous that to place a trap at each is impossible. In states where groundhogs (woodchucks), are numerous there are often a hundred or more dens along a single bluff or rocky bank. To have enough steel traps to set one at each is something few trappers do, yet two or three deadfalls in connection with a line of steel traps is all that is necessary and the trapper can move on to the next bluff where dens are numerous and set another trap or two. As a rule it is where there are many dens, close together, that deadfalls make the best catches, yet when you find a good den anywhere, set or construct a deadfall.

All trappers have noticed when tracking animals in the snow that they visit nearly every den along their route, not always going in but just sticking their head in. When thus investigating, the animal smells the bait and is hungry (as nine times out of ten the animal is hunting something to eat), and if your trap is set properly you are reasonably sure to make a catch.

In the North, Canada, Alaska and some of the states on the Canadian border where trapping is made a business, it is no uncommon thing for one man to have as many as one hundred and fifty traps and some have out twice that many, or three hundred. Marten trappers in the trackless forests often blaze out a route fifty or more miles in length, building shelters along the line where nights are spent.

The trapper who only spends a few hours each day at trapping and lives in thickly settled districts will find that it is hard for him to locate suitable places perhaps for more than thirty to fifty traps, yet if these will be looked at properly during the season the catch will justify the time and labor in building.

The number of deadfalls and snares that each trapper should construct in his section must largely be determined by himself, depending upon how large a territory he has to trap over without running into other trappers' grounds. It will be little use to build traps where there are other trappers as trouble will occur, traps may be torn to pieces, etc. Yet there are many good places to build traps in your immediate locality no doubt. If there are any creeks near and woods along the banks you will find good places at both creek and in the woods. If in sections where there is no forest, like some western states, deadfalls trapping may be difficult from the fact that there is nothing to build them with.

In such cases the portable traps, (described elsewhere) in this book, can probably be used to advantage, but best of all in such places is steel traps.

The number of deadfalls and snares that a trapper can attend to is large, from the fact that the game is killed and as the weather is usually cold, the traps need not be looked at only about twice each week.

In the North, many trappers have such long lines that they do not get over them only once a week. The trouble where deadfalls are only looked at once in seven days is that other animals are apt to find the game and may injure the fur, or even destroy the pelt.

Where snares with spring pole attachment are used, and the weather is cold, the trapper need not make the rounds only once a week, as all animals will be suspended in the air and out of the reach of flesh eaters.

South of 40 degrees where the weather is not severe, it is policy to look at traps at least twice a week, and in the extreme South the trapper should make his rounds every day.

It will thus be seen that a trapper in the North can attend more deadfalls and snares than one in the South or even in the Central States. No trapper should have more traps or longer lines than he can properly attend to. The fur bearing animals are none too numerous without having them caught and their pelts and fur spoiled before the arrival of the trapper.

89

CHAPTER XXII

WHEN TO TRAP

The proper season to begin trapping is when cold weather comes. The old saying that fur is good any month that has an "r" in does not hold good except in the North. Even there September is too early to begin, yet muskrat and skunk are worth something as well as other furs. In the spring April is the last month with an "r." In most sections muskrat, bear, beaver, badger and otter are good all thru April, but other animals began shedding weeks before.

The rule for trappers to follow is to put off trapping in the fall until nights are frosty and the ground freezes.

Generally speaking in Canada and the more Northern States trappers can begin about November 1 and should cease March 1, with the exception of water animals, bear and badger, which may be trapped a month later. In the Central and Southern States trappers should not begin so early and should leave off in the spring from one to four weeks sooner — depending upon how far South they are located.

At the interior Hudson Bay posts, where their word is law, October 25 is appointed to begin and May 25th to quit hunting and trapping with the exception of bear, which are considered prime up to June 10. Remember that the above dates are for the interior or Northern H. B. Posts, which are located hundreds of miles north of the boundary between the United States and Canada.

The skunk is the first animal to become prime, then the coon, marten, fisher, mink and fox, but the latter does not become strictly prime until after a few days of snow, says an old Maine trapper. Rats and beaver are late in priming up as well as otter and mink, and tho the mink is not strictly a land animal, it becomes prime about with the later land animals. The bear, which is strictly a land animal, is not in good fur until snow comes and not strictly prime until February or March.

With the first frosts and cool days many trappers begin setting and baiting their traps. That it is easier to catch certain kinds of fur-bearing animals early in the season is known to most trappers and for this reason trapping in most localities is done too early in the season.

Some years ago when trapping was done even earlier than now, we examined mink skins that were classed as No. 4 and worth 10 or 15 cents, that, had they been allowed to live a few weeks longer, their hides would have been No. 1 and worth, according to locality, from $1.50 to $3.50 each. This early trapping is a loss to the trapper if they will only pause and think. There are only so many animals in a locality to be caught each winter and why catch them before their fur is prime?

In the latitude of Southern Ohio, Indiana, Illinois, etc., skunk caught in the month of October are graded back from one to three grades (and even sometimes into trash), where if they were not caught until November 15th how different would be the classification. The same is true of opossum, mink, muskrat, coon, fox, etc.

Skunk are one of the animals that become prime first each fall. The date that they become prime depends much on the weather. Fifteen years ago, when trapping in Southern Ohio, the writer has sold skunk at winter prices caught as early as October 16, while other seasons those caught the 7th of November, or three weeks later, blued and were graded back. Am glad to say that years ago I learned not to put out traps until November.

That the weather has much to do with the priming of furs and pelts there is no question. If the fall is colder than usual the furs will become prime sooner, while if the freezing weather is later the pelts will be later in "priming up."

In the sections where weasel turn white (then called ermine by many), trappers have a good guide. When they become white they are prime and so are most other land animals. In fact, some are fairly good a week or two before.

When a pelt is put on the stretcher and becomes blue in a few days it is far from prime and will grade no better than No. 2. If the pelt turns black the chances are that the pelt will grade No. 3 or 4, In the case of mink, when dark spots only appear on the pelt, it is not quite prime.

Trappers and hunters should remember that no pelt is prime or No. 1 when it turns the least blue. Opossum skins seldom turn blue even if caught early — most other skins do.

CHAPTER XXIII

SEASON'S CATCH

The reason that many trappers make small catches, each season, is from the fact that they spend only an hour or so each day at trapping, while at most other business the party devotes the entire day. The trapper who looks out his grounds some weeks in advance of the trapping season is not idling his time away. He should also have a line of traps constructed in advance of the trapping season.

There is a fascination connected with trapping that fills one with a strange feeling when all alone constructing deadfalls and snares or on the rounds to see what success has been yours. I have often visited traps of old trappers, where from two to five carcasses were hanging from a nearby sapling.

There are several instances on record where two animals have been caught in one deadfall at the same time. A well-known trapper of Ohio claims to have caught three skunk in one deadfall at one time a few years since. Whether such is an actual fact or not we are unable to say. The cases on record where two animals have been caught are so well substantiated that there is little room left to doubt the truth of same.

The catching of two animals at the same time is not such an extraordinary occurrence as many, at first, think. If two animals should come along at the same time and, smelling the bait, begin a meal, the result is easily seen.

While trapping with deadfalls is a humane way of catching fur-bearing animals, another thing in their favor is that skunk are usually killed without "perfuming" themselves, trap and trapper as well. Then, again, if once caught, there is no getting away.

Trappers in the forest always have the necessary tools, axe or heavy hatchet and knife, with which to build a deadfall, while their steel traps may all be exhausted and none set within miles. A deadfall is built and perhaps on the trapper's return an animal is lying dead between the poles.

During extreme cold weather there is but little use to look at traps set for skunk, raccoon, etc., as they do not travel. Before a thaw or warm spell the entire line should be gone over and all old bait removed and replaced with fresh bait.

Like many another trapper you will visit your traps time after time without catching much if any fur, yet if your traps are properly constructed and are spread over a large area, you will catch considerable fur during the season.

Deadfalls and snares can he strung out for miles and while they should be looked at every other day, in good trapping weather, they can be neglected, if the trapper cannot get around more than twice a week, without game escaping. If you visit your traps frequently there will be no loss from injury to fur. While it is true, should a small animal be caught in a heavy trap, one built for much larger game, it will be considerably flattened out, yet the skin or fur is not damaged. There is nothing to damage your catch, in most sections, unless you do not visit your traps often enough in warm weather, when they may be faintly tainted. Most trapping is done, however, in cool weather, but occasionally there may come a warm spell when skins become tainted. If found in such condition skin as soon as possible and place upon boards or stretchers.

Another thing greatly to the advantage of the deadfall and snare trapper is the fact that a trapper never knows just when he will be able to visit his traps again; the unexpected often happens, and should it be a day or so longer than expected the deadfall or snare still securely holds the game.

As all experienced trappers know, the first night of a cold spell is a splendid one for animals to travel (they seem forewarned about the weather) and a good catch is the result. If the trapper is a "weather prophet" his traps are all freshly baited and in order, for this is the time that game is on the move — often looking up new and warm dens and generally hungry. Should the next days be cold and stormy the trapper should get over the line as promptly as possible. After once getting over the line after the "cold spell," it is not so important that traps be looked at for some days again.

The successful trapper will always be on the watch of the weather. Some animals, it is true, travel during the coldest weather, but there are many that do not, so that the trapper who sees that his deadfalls are freshly baited when the signs point to warmer weather. After days and nights of severe weather most animals are hungry and when the weather moderates they are on the move.

"I have more than one hundred deadfalls and catch large numbers of skunk," writes a Connecticut trapper. "A few years ago a trapper within two miles of here caught more than 60 coon in deadfalls. Since then coon have been rather scarce, but I am going to try them this coming fall. I prefer red squirrel for skunk bait to anything else, and extract of valerian for scent. Try it, trapper — it can't be beat. I have used it for twenty years and can catch my share every time."

The trapper that makes the largest catches usually is the one that has deadfalls and snares in addition to steel traps. Recently two trappers wrote of their season's catch and added that a good proportion was caught in deadfalls and snares. These trappers were located in Western Canada; marten 54, lynx 12, mink 19, ermine 71, wild cat 11, foxes 18.

While these trappers did not say, it is presumed that the foxes were caught in snares or steel traps, for it is seldom that one is caught in a deadfall. In Canada and the New England States, where foxes are plentiful, the snare is used to a considerable extent.

Skunk, mink, ermine, weasel and opossum are easily caught in deadfalls. One trapper in a southern state is said to have caught 94 mink, besides 38 coon and 57 opossum, in 28 deadfalls, from November 25th to February 25th, or three months.

CHAPTER XXIV

GENERAL INFORMATION

Early in September, 1906, the editor spent a couple of days at his home in Southern Ohio, where in the '80's along and near a small stream known as Kyger Creek, considerable trapping was done.

If readers are curious and have a good, large map of Ohio, and look at the southern border, some fifty miles above the mouth of the Scioto river, on a direct line or about double that by following the winding of the river, they will find Kyger Creek. The stream is about ten miles long and empties into the Ohio river below the village of Cheshire. The country is rather rough and rocky, but the timber has mainly disappeared.

A quarter of a century ago, opossum, muskrat, skunk, and fox were more numerous than now. Mink at that time were few, but in the early '80's they seemed to become fairly plentiful all at once. The high price has caused considerable trapping, and their number has decreased of recent years.

In trapping we found deadfalls, properly made, set and baited to be an excellent trap for mink, skunk and opossum. As there were few coon where we were trapping, but few were caught, yet an old trapper nearby caught several in both deadfalls and steel traps each season.

There is no doubt but that a trapper who expects to remain months at the same place should have a few deadfalls. These traps, like steel traps, to make catches, do not depend upon numbers so much as correct and careful construction and setting. A half dozen deadfalls located at the right places, carefully built and properly set, are worth probably as much as fifty carelessly constructed and located at haphazard.

Some object to deadfalls because fox are seldom caught in them. It is true that few fox are taken in deadfalls, although in the far North some are, and especially Arctic and White fox.

The deadfall trapper, however, who gives care and attention to his traps finds them fur takers. They can be built small for weasel or a little larger for mink, marten and civet cat; or larger for opossum and skunk; still heavier for coon and wild cat and even to a size that kills bear.

Some trappers find the mink hard to catch. At some seasons they are easy to take in deadfalls. Long in the '80's in five winters eight mink were caught in one deadfall. The first winter one was caught; second, two; third, three; fourth and fifth, each one.

If our memory serves us right, the trap was first built in the fall of 1887, and was located on the bank about ten feet to the left of a sycamore, which at that time was standing. There was a den under the tree entering near the water, with an outlet on the bank only a few feet from the trap, and near where the pen and bait were located.

This deadfall was built much like the illustration shown here. While the fall was of hickory, not a vestige remained when looking at the place in September, 1906.

The pen should be built strong and tight so that the animal will not tear it to pieces and get at the bait from the rear. The "fall" or top pole can be of any kind of wood, but hickory, oak, beech, maple, and other heavy wood are all good. The pole should be heavy enough to kill the animal without placing any weights on it. When building it is a good idea to let the top pole extend about a couple of feet beyond the pen. This will give more weight on the animal when the trap falls.

A GOOD CATCHER

The two piece triggers may work hard, especially if the log used for the fall has rough bark on. In this case it might be well to smooth with your axe or hatchet. In setting with the two piece trigger make them out of as hard wood as can be found. The long piece can be slightly flattened on the under side, or the side on which the upper end of the upright or prop sets. The prop should be cut square on the lower end while the upper end might be a little rounding, as this will tend to make the top or bait trigger slip off easier.

In setting raise up the top pole and hold in position with the knee. This gives both hands free to adjust the triggers. When you think you have them right, gradually let the weight off your knee and then try the trigger. You will soon learn about how they are to be set.

The bait should be tied on or the bait trigger may have a prong on to hold the bait. If you find the bait gone and the trap still up the chances are that it was set too hard and the animal stole the bait.

Of late years in some sections, mice have been very troublesome, eating the bait. In other places birds are bait stealers, and for this reason it is best to set traps rather hard to throw.

The location of a deadfall has much to do with the catch. Old trappers know if they were to set a steel trap in a place not frequented by fur bearers that their catch would be next to nothing. The same applies to all sets, whether steel traps, snares or deadfalls.

In the illustration it will be noticed that the opening or the side which the animal enters for bait is facing the creek. When building these traps it will be found best to leave the open side toward the water if trapping for mink or coon, as they generally leave the edge of the water going directly to dens along and near the bank.

The under log in the deadfall shown does not extend but a few inches beyond the two end stakes. It should extend eight or ten inches beyond. The four stakes at pen must be of sufficient length that when the trap is set they extend above the top or fall pole. If they did not, the trap in falling, might catch on the end of one of the stakes and not go down.

Along streams these traps need not be close. A couple to the mile is plenty. Of course, if there are places where dens are numerous more can be built to advantage, while along other stretches of water it may be useless to build them at all. It all depends upon whether animals travel there. You cannot catch them in any kind of trap if they are not there.

For opossum, skunk, mink, civet cat, coon, ermine, etc., find where the animals live or where they go frequently searching for food. If building where there are dens, either locate within a few feet of the one that appears best or just off the path that the animal takes in going from one to the other. Have the open part next to path and say only three feet off.

Marten trappers, while placing traps on high ground, do not pay so much attention to dens and paths, for these animals spend much time in trees looking for squirrels, birds, etc., but go through the forest "spotting a line" and locate a deadfall in likely ground about every 200 yards, or about 8 to the mile.

CHAPTER XXV

SKINNING AND STRETCHING

Much importance should be attached to the skinning and stretching of all kinds of skins so as to command the highest commercial value. The fisher, otter, foxes, lynx, marten, mink, ermine, civet, cats and skunk should be cased, that is, taken off whole.

Commence with the knife in the center of one hind foot and slit up the inside of the leg, up to and around the vent and down the other leg in a like manner. Cut around the vent, taking care not to cut the lumps or glands in which the musk of certain animals is secreted, then strip the skin from the bone of the tail with the aid of a split stick gripped firmly in the hand while the thumb of the other hand presses against the animals back just above. Make no other slits in the skin except in the case of the skunk and otter, whose tails require to be split, spread, and tacked on a board.

Turn the skin back over the body, leaving the pelt side out and the fur side inward, and by cutting a few ligaments, it will peel off very readily. Care should be taken to cut closely around the nose, ears and lips, so as not to tear the skin. Have a board made about the size and shape of the three-board stretcher, only not split in halves. This board is to put the skin over in order to hold it better while removing particles of fat and flesh which adheres to it while skinning, which can be done with a blunt-edged knife, by scraping the skin from the tail down toward the nose — the direction in which the hair roots grow — never scrape up the other way or you will injure the fiber of the skin, and care should be taken not to scrape too hard, for if the skin fiber is injured its value is decreased.

Now, having been thoroughly "fleshed," as the above process is called, the skin is ready for stretching, which is done by inserting the two halves of the three-board stretcher and drawing the skin over the boards to its fullest extent, with the back on one side and the belly on the other, and tacking it fast by driving in a small nail an inch or so from each side of the tail near the edges of the skin; also, in like manner the other side. Now insert the wedge and drive it between the halves almost its entire length. Care should be taken, however, to not stretch the skin so much as to make the fur appear thin and thus injure its value. Now put a nail in the root of the tail and fasten it to the wedge; also, draw up all slack parts and fasten. Care should be taken to have both sides of the skin of equal length, which can be done by lapping the leg flippers over each other. Now draw up the under lip and fasten, and pull the nose down until it meets the lip and tack it fast, and then the skin is ready to hang away to cure.

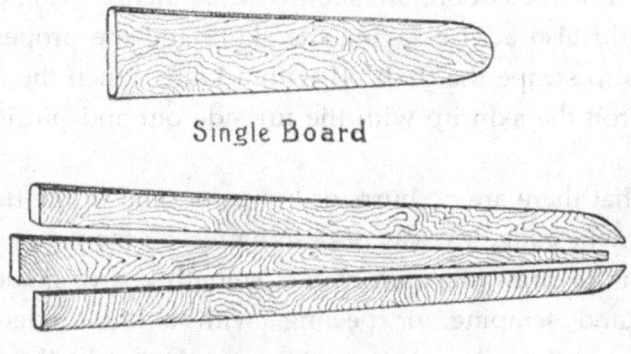

Single Board

Three Board Stretcher

SINGLE AND THREE BOARD STRETCHER

Do not dry skins at a fire or in the sun, or in smoke. It often burns them when they will not dress and are of no value. Dry in a well-covered shed or tent where there is a free circulation of air, and never use any preparation, such as alum and salt, as it only injures them for market. Never stretch the noses out long, as some trappers are inclined to do, but treat them as above described, and they will command better values. Fur buyers are inclined to class long-nosed skins as "southern" and pay a small price for them, as Southern skins are much lighter in fur than those of the North.

The badger, beaver, bear, raccoon and wolf must always be skinned "open;" that is, ripped up the belly from vent to chin after

101

the following manner: Cut across the hind legs as if to be "cased" and then rip up the belly. The skin can then be removed by flaying as in skinning a beef.

Another experienced trapper says: The animals which should be skinned open are bear, beaver, raccoon, badger, timber wolf and wolverines. The way to do this is to rip the skin open from the point of the lower jaw, in a straight line, to the vent. Then rip it open on the back of the hind legs, and the inside of the front legs, and peel the skin carefully off the body. Beaver, however, should not have the front legs split open and the tail, having no fur, is of course cut off. If the skin is a fine one, and especially in the case of bear, the feet should not be cut off, but should be skinned, leaving the claws on. I would also advise saving the skull, and the proper way to clean it is to scrape the flesh off with a knife. When the animal is skinned, roll the skin up with the fur side out and put it in your pack.

See that there are no burrs or lumps of mud in the fur, before you do any fleshing. My way of fleshing furs — there may be better ways — is to draw the skin over a smooth board, made for the purpose and scraping, or peeling, with a blunt edged knife. Commence at the tail, and scrape towards the head, otherwise you may injure the fibre of the hide. Over the back and shoulders of most animals is a thin layer of flesh. This should be removed, and when done, there should be nothing remaining but the skin and fur. Raccoon and muskrat are easily fleshed by pinching the flesh between the edge of the knife and the thumb.

For stretching boards, I prefer a three board stretcher, but a plain board will answer. For muskrats, use a single board. Open skins are best stretched in frames or hoops, but it is all right to stretch them on the wall on the inside of a building. The boards shown in the cut are, to my notion, the proper shapes, and I would advise making a good supply of them before the season commences.

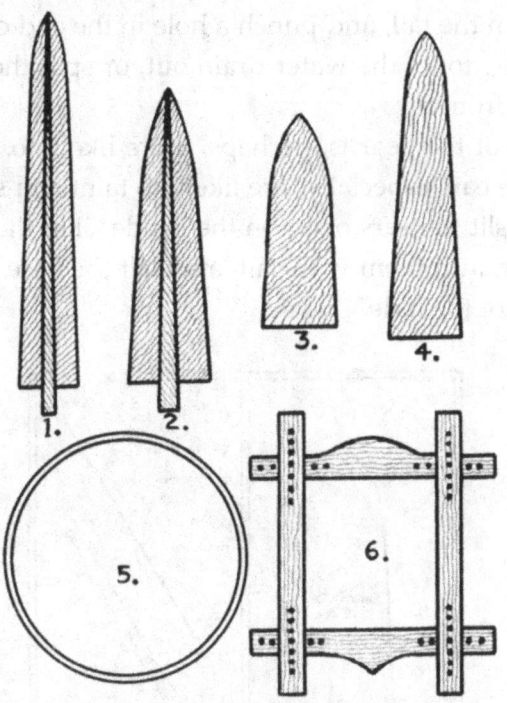

SOME STRETCHING PATTERNS

To use these three board stretchers, insert the two halves of the board in the skin, draw the skin down and fasten the hind legs, with tacks, to the edges of the boards. This stretches the hide long. Then insert the wedge between the two boards, which will stretch the skin out to its fullest extent, and give it the proper shape. Finish by fastening with tacks, pulling the nose over the point of the board, and drawing the skin of the lower jaw up against the nose. Hang the furs in a cool, dry place and as soon as they are dry, remove them from the boards. Fox skins should be turned with the fur side out, after removing from the board.

In using the hoop stretcher, the hide is laced inside the hoop, with twine, the skin of the coon being stretched square and the beaver round. All other furs should be stretched so as not to draw them out of their natural shape. If the weather is warm and the furs are likely to taint, salt them. A salted skin is better than a tainted one. Put salt in the tail, and punch a hole in the end of the tail, with a pointed wire, to let the water drain out, or split the tail up about one-half inch from tip.

The skin of the bear is, perhaps, more likely to spoil than any other, and the ears especially, are likely to taint and slip the fur. To prevent this, slit the ears open on the inside, skin then back almost to the edge and fill them with salt, also salt the base of the ears, on the flesh side of the hide.

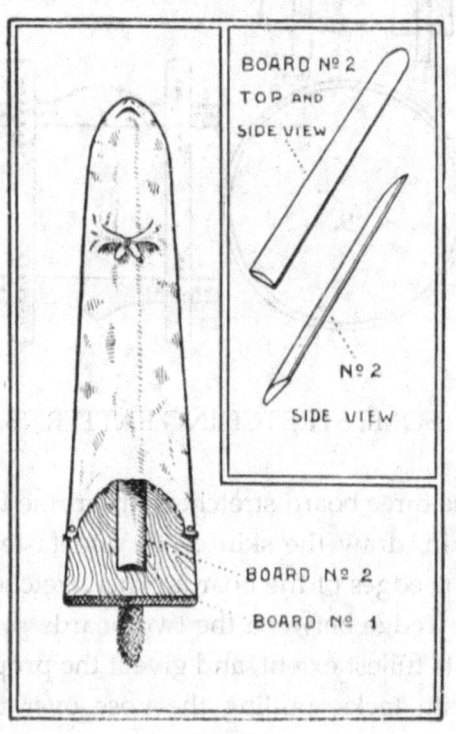

DAKOTA TRAPPERS' METHOD

In stretching, says a North Dakota trapper, we use a one board stretcher as follows: Put on the fur after you have fleshed it, the four feet on one side and the tail on the other. Tack down the hind feet and the tail, then take a piece of board about 1 x 1/4 inches (this would be about the correct size for a mink) rounded off except on one side. Put it below the fur on the side where the feet are, tie the front feet. When you are going to take off the fur, pull out the small board and the fur will come off easy.

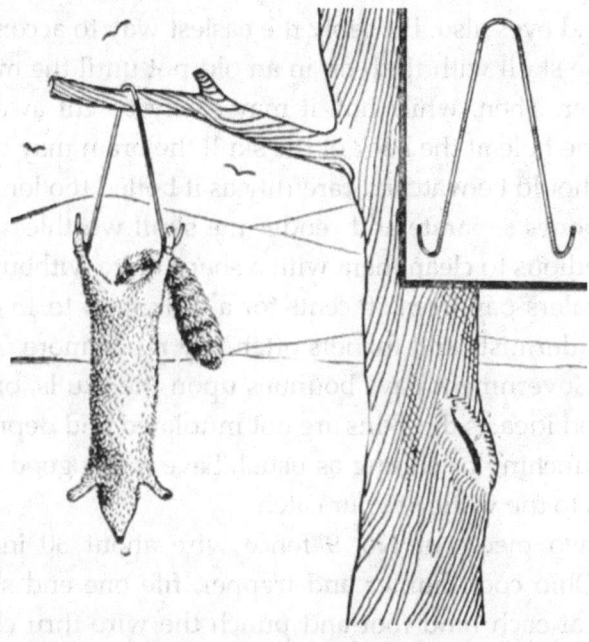

HOLDER FOR SKINNING

A contrivance which I have found useful in skinning is made of a piece of stiff wire 18 inches long. Bend this at the middle until it has the shape of V with the ends about 8 inches apart. Bend up an inch at each end to form a hook and when skinning, after cutting around the hind feet, hook into the large tendons, hang on a nail or over limb, etc., and go ahead with both hands. The wire must be nearly as large as a slate pencil and will work all right from foxes down to mink. Trappers will find this a great help in skinning animals after they have become cold. Young trappers should use this simple device as they will be less liable to cut holes in the skin. It pays to be careful in skinning animals properly as well as to stretch them correctly, for both add to their market value.

How many trappers save the skulls of their larger game? All the skulls of bear, puma or mountain lion, wolves, foxes and sometimes those of lynx and wild cat are of ready sale if they contain good sets of teeth. Several parties buy these skulls for cash.

To prepare them the bulk of the flesh should be removed and the brain and eyes also. Probably the easiest way to accomplish this is to boil the skull with flesh on in an old pot until the meat begins to get tender. Then, while hot, it may easily be cut away, and by enlarging the hole at the back of the skull the brain may be scooped out. They should be watched carefully as if boiled too long the teeth drop out, bones separate and render the skull worthless. It is safe, but more tedious to clean them with a sharp knife without boiling.

The dealers pay from 50 cents for a bear skull to 15 cents for a fox, tho taxidermists and furriers often pay much more. The British Columbia Government pays bounties upon the skulls, only I think this is a good idea as the skins are not mutilated and depreciated by scalping, punching or cutting as usual. Save a few good skulls and add dollars to the value of your catch.

Take two pieces of No. 9 fence wire about 30 inches long, writes an Ohio coon hunter and trapper, file one end sharp, then commence at each hind foot and punch the wire thru close to the edge as in sewing, taking stitches an inch or so long until you get to the front foot, then pull the hide along the wire just far enough so the top and bottom will stretch out to make it square, or a few inches longer than the width is better.

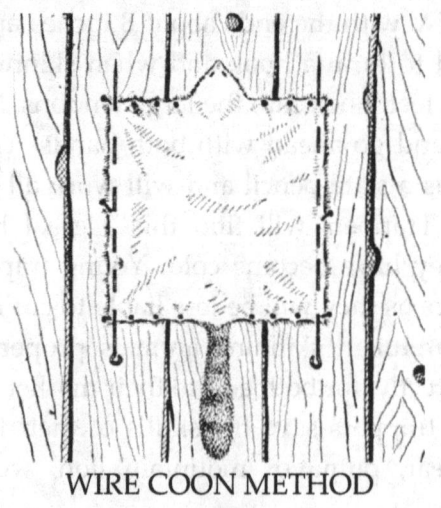

WIRE COON METHOD

Put 3 or 4 nails in each side, then commence at the top and tack all but the head, then pull the bottom down even with the sides, not tacking the head, which lets it draw down into the hide, then tack the head. This is an easy and good way to handle coon skins making them nearly square when stretched.

Many inexperienced trappers stretch coon skins too long and draw out the head and neck. This can be avoided by following instructions given here. Coon can be cased but most dealers prefer to have them stretched open.

Get a lot of steel wire, says a Missouri trapper who uses old umbrella wires, the round solid ones. Sharpen one end, take your coon skin and run one wire up each side and one across each end.

In putting these wires in do it like the old woman knits, that is, wrap the hide around the wire and stick it thru about every inch. Now cut six small twigs, make them the proper length and notch the ends, and you will soon have your hide stretched expert trapper style.

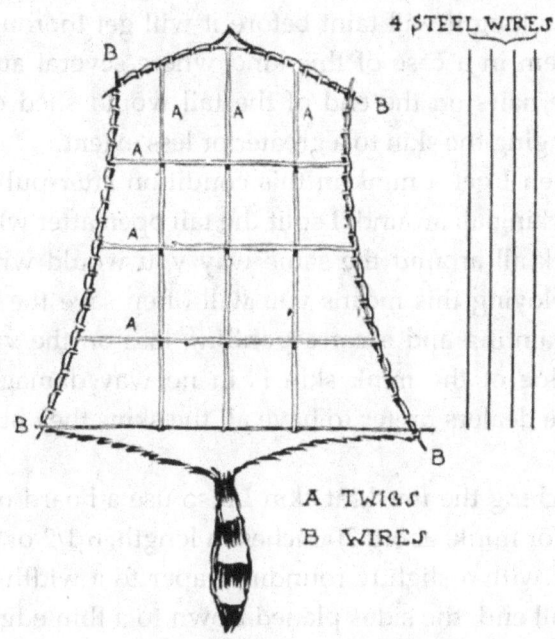

WIRE AND TWIG COON METHOD

The advantage of this is you can carry stretchers enough for twenty-five skins in one hand and don't have to hunt up a barn door and box of tacks and hammer every time you want to stretch one. You can stretch in one-fourth the time it would take to tack up on a board, and you will have it in first class style the first time and not have to pull out a tack here and stretch a little more there.

I have always used the whole board (not split into two pieces and wedged shape piece as some do), writes a Massachusetts trapper, and made as follows:

For mink I use a 3/8 inch board about 40 inches in length, 4 inches wide at the large end, tapering to about 2 1/2 inches at the small end with the edges planed down from near the middle of the board to the edge, leaving a thin edge and sandpapered down smooth. I make the board of this length for the reason that it sometimes happens that a mink may have laid in a trap for several days before being taken out, and if under water it is not always easy to determine the exact length of time it has been in the trap, and there may be a possibility that if put on the board to dry that having laid so long it will taint before it will get thoroughly dry. I have seen them in a case of this kind where several and perhaps nearly all the hairs on the end of the tail would shed or pull out thereby damaging the skin to a greater or less extent.

Now when I get a mink in this condition after pulling on the board and tacking all around, I split the tail open after which I lay it open and tack all around the same way you would with an otter skin. By employing this means you will often save the loss of the tail by thus tainting and a corresponding loss on the value of the skin. The value of the mink skin is in no way damaged by this process. Some dealers prefer to have all the skins they buy cured in this manner.

For stretching the muskrat skin I also use a board of the same thickness as for mink, about 20 inches in length, 6 1/2 or 7 inches at the large end with a slightly rounding taper to a width of about 3 inches at small end, the sides planed down to a thin edge the same as for the mink boards; in fact, I prefer the same manner of stretching all cased skins, using care not to have the boards so wide as to stretch the skins to a width much exceeding the natural width before it was placed over the board, but giving them all the strain they will stand with reason, lengthwise. If stretched too wide it tends to make the fur thinner and lessens the value of it.

I usually pull the skins, especially muskrats, onto the boards far enough so that the smaller end will extend through the mouth of the skin for perhaps 1/2 inch, and when the skins are sufficiently dry to remove, all that is required is to take hold of them with a hand on either edge of the skin and give it a sharp tap on the small end, when the skin will come off at once. By stretching the skins on the boards with the back on one side, belly on the opposite side, they come off the boards looking smooth and uniform in width, and command a great deal better price than if thrown on in a haphazard way on a shingle or an inch board badly shaped, as a great many beginners do. I have seen some shameful work done in this respect.

It is always necessary to remove all surplus grease and fat which can readily be done immediately after the skin is stretched, otherwise they will heat, sweat and mold to a certain extent after they are removed from the boards, which injures both the appearance and sale of them. It is well to look after all these little details. These descriptions are given with the desire to help some of the beginners. If they will start in by using a little care in stretching and having pride in their work they will find the business both more pleasant and profitable.

If convenient when going into camp, writes an old successful trapper who has pursued the fur bearers in many states, you should take several stretching boards for your different kinds of fur with you. If not, you can generally find a tree that will split good and you can split some out. It is usually hard to find widths that are long and straight enough to bend so as to form a good shaped stretcher. You should always aim to stretch and cure furs you catch in the best manner.

In skinning you should rip the animal straight from one heel across to the other and close to the roots of the tail on the under side. Work the skin loose around the bone at the base until you can

109

grasp the bone of the tail with the first two fingers of the right hand while you place the bone between the first two fingers of the left hand. Then, by pulling you will draw the entire bone from the tail which you should always do.

Sometimes when the animal has been dead for some time the bone will not readily draw from the tail. In this case cut a stick the size of your finger about eight inches long. Cut it away in the center until it will readily bend so that the two ends will come together. Then cut a notch in each part of stick just large enough to let the bone of the tail in and squeeze it out. It is necessary to whittle one side of the stick at the notch so as to form a square shoulder.

You should have about three sizes of stretching boards for mink and fox. For mink they should be from 4 1/2 inches down to 3 inches and for fox from 6 1/4 inches down to 5 inches wide, and in length the fox boards may be four feet long, and the mink boards three feet long.

The boards should taper slightly down to within 8 inches of the end for fox, and then rounded up to a round point. The mink boards should be rounded at 4 or 5 inches from this point. You will vary the shape of the board in proportion to the width. Stretching boards should not be more than 3/8 inch thick. A belly strip the length or nearly the length of the boards 1 1/4 inches at the wide end, tapering to a point at the other end and about 1/4 to 3/8 inch thick. Have the boards smooth and even on the edges. Other stretching boards should be made in proportion to the size and shape of the animal whose skin is to be stretched.

You should not fail to remove all the fat and flesh from the skin immediately after the skin is on the board. If a skin is wet when taken from the animal it should be drawn lightly on a board until the fur is quite dry. Then turn the skin flesh side out and stretch.

Beginning at the left, dimensions and skins stretched on the various boards are given:

No. 1. Mink board, length 28 inches and 4 wide.

No. 2. Mink board, length 28 inches and 3 1/2 wide.

No. 3. Weasel board length 20 inches and 2 1/2 wide.

No. 4. Muskrat board, length 21 inches and 6 inches wide.

110

No. 5. Opossum board, (small), length 20 inches and 6 1/2 inches wide.

No. 6. Skunk or opossum, (medium), length 28 inches and 7 inches wide.

No. 7. Skunk and opossum, (large), length 28 inches and 8 inches wide.

SIZE OF STRETCHING BOARDS

Old and experienced hunters and trappers know about the shape and size to make the various stretching boards for the fur bearers, but for the guidance of beginners and those who are careless about stretching pelts, the above description is especially meant.

Trappers in Southern sections will no doubt find the boards as described here too large for most of their skunk. In the Northeast the mink boards will also be too large, but for this section (Ohio), they are about correct. The general shape of the boards can be seen from the illustration.

One of the best ways, writes a Minnesota trapper, to take off the skin of an animal is by cutting the skin around the hind legs or feet, and then slitting the skin down inside the hind legs to the body joining the two slits between the hind legs, then remove the skin on the tail by pushing up the thumb nail, or a thin flat piece of wood against the bone of the tail and draw off the skin.

Now commence to draw the body of the animal through the slit already made without enlarging it, drawing the skin over itself, the fur side within. When the forefeet are reached, cut the skin away from them at the wrists, and then skin over the head until the mouth is reached when the skin should be finally removed at the lips.

One thing to be borne in mind when stretching a skin to dry, is that it must be drawn tight; another, that it must be stretched in a place where neither the heat of a fire or that of the sun will reach it too strongly, and it should not be washed. Large skins may be nailed on a wall of a shed or barn.

The board stretcher should be made of some thin material. Prepare a board of bass wood or some other light material, two feet three inches long, three inches and a half wide at one end, and two inches and an eighth at the other, and three-eighths of an inch thick. Chamfer it from the center to the sides almost to an edge. Round and chamfer the small end about an inch upon the sides. Split the board through the center with a knife or saw, finally prepare a wedge of the same length and thickness, one inch wide at the large end, and taper to a blunt point. This is a stretcher suitable for a mink, or a marten.

Two large sizes with similar proportions are required for the large animals, the largest size suitable for the full grown otter and wolf, should be five feet and a half long, seven inches wide at the large end when fully spread by the wedge, and six inches at the small end. An intermediate size is required for the fisher, raccoon, fox and some other animals, the proportions of which can be easily figured out.

These stretchers require that the skin of the animal should not be ripped through the belly, but should be stripped off whole. Peel the skin from the body by drawing it over itself, leaving the fur

112

inward. In this condition the skin should be drawn on to the split board (with the back on one side and the belly on the other), to its utmost length, and fastened with tacks, and then the wedge should be driven between the two halves. Finally, make all fast by a tack at the root of the tail, and another on the opposite side. The skin is then stretched to its utmost capacity and it may be hung away to dry.

Not alone the skulls of the larger animals, but the skulls of any game, the skeleton of any bird, or fish, has a ready market, provided such specimens are properly cleaned, and in perfect condition. However, the hunter or trapper must bear in mind the fact that it is the perfect specimen that is in demand, and that a bruise on the bone literally spoils it for the curator.

If you will look carefully at any skull, you will notice that some of the bones are very thin and frail, almost like a spider web. These fine bones must be preserved if they are to be of any value to the Comparative Anatomist, and boiling or scraping simply ruins them. So much for the explanation. Now the method of cleaning, is by "rotting" rather than scraping or boiling. Take the skull (or whole head) and fix it solid in some can or jar, then fill it, or cover with water and put away for three or four weeks. At the end of that time, pour off the water and the bulk of the flesh will go too. Fill in with clear water again, and repeat as often as necessary. I have found that twice will do the work, and leave the bone in good condition.

There is a market for most animal skulls, if not damaged, and it may pay to preserve all. In the Hunter-Trader-Trapper, published at Columbus, Ohio, usually will be found advertisements of parties who buy them.

I have never had much luck with two-piece stretchers, but use thin board stretchers in one piece with a "sword stick" on each side to fully stretch and admit the air to both sides of the skin. This cures the skin faster and better than when only one side is exposed to the air, says a Maryland trapper.

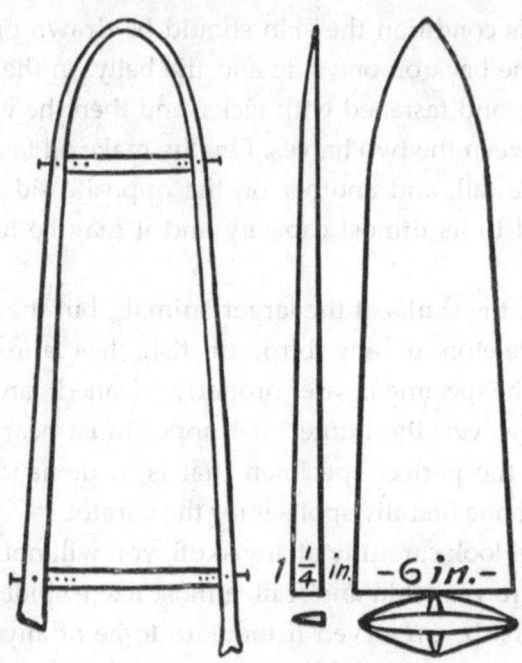

$1\frac{1}{4}$ in. -6 in.-

POLE STRETCHERS

When off from home, I use stretchers made from saplings, as boards suitable are not to be had everywhere, and cannot be bothered with when going light. To make these, cut osier, willow or hickory switches, straight and thick as the finger, about four feet long; cut two short pieces for rats 4 and 6 inches long and carefully bending the long piece. Nail these in with a small wire nail at each end. A handful of shingle or lath nails and a clump of osier sprouts will make a full outfit of stretchers for a temporary camp.

I know it is as much value in stretching your furs and preparing them for market as it is in trapping, writes a trapper. If you have no boards, go to your grocer or dry goods store and you can get all the boxes you want for 5 or 10 cents apiece. They must not be over 3/8 of an inch thick; if they are, plane them down smooth on both sides.

I make what I call the two piece stretcher with a wedge for muskrats. Take a board 20 inches long, 3/8 inch thick, 6 inches wide large end, 2 1/2 inches small end. Taper back 5 inches from small end. Now take block plane and chaffer off each side an inch or more up and round it off. Round and chaffer small end the same, almost to an edge. Now draw a line thru the center of the board and saw it thru.

Make a wedge the same length and thickness, 3/8 of an inch wide and tapering down to 1/10 of an inch. If a large skin, push it in between the halves. Bore a hole in large end and hang up in a cool ventilated place to dry. After three days pull out wedge, and your fur will slip right off without tearing. If the boards should warp over, tack a strip across the large end.

The mink stretchers are made on the same plan. A board the same thickness, 30 inches long, 3 1/2 inches wide, taper down 2 1/8 small end round chaffer. For large mink insert wedge made one inch wide. Taper down to 2/8. For skunk and coon they are also good, only they are made on a larger scale.

Now a word about casing. Pull your hide on so the back is on one side and the belly on the other. Pull nose over small end 1/2 inch. Put two tacks on each side, now pull down tight to large end and put two tacks each side, lay board on bench and take an old case knife, scrape off all meat and fat and be careful not to scrape too thin, so as not to cut the fibre of the skin. After you have scraped the flesh off, insert the wedge and your skin will be tight. Do not stretch your hide so it will make your fur look thin.

This is my way of stretching coon hide; use four-penny nails and use either the inside or outside of some old building, inside is the best. Drive the first nail thru nose. This holds the hide for starting. Pull each forward leg up (not out) on a level with nose and about seven or eight inches from nose according to size of the coon. Drive next nail at root of tail, and pull down, moderately tight.

Now pull each hind leg out about one inch wider than the fore legs and a little below the tail nail. Now use a nail every inch and pull the hide up between the forward legs and nose, until it comes straight across. Next, treat the bottom of the hide the same as the top. Use plenty of nails. To finish down the sides, drive a nail first on one side and then on the other until finished. You will find when done that the hide is nearly square with no legs sticking out the sides and no notches in the skin.

CHAPTER XXVI

HANDLING AND GRADING

MINK should be cased fur side in and stretched on boards for several days or until dry.

SKUNK should be cased fur side in and stretched on boards for several days. The white stripe cut out, blackened, etc., reduces the value.

RACCOON should be stretched open (ripped up the belly) and nailed on boards or the inside of a building. Some dealers allow as much for coon cased, from any section, while others prefer that only Southern coon be cased.

FOXES of the various kinds should be cased and put on boards fur side in for a few days, or until dry. As the pelt is thin they soon dry, when they must be taken off and should be turned fur side out. In shipping see that they are not packed against furs flesh side out.

LYNX should be cased and after drying properly are turned fur side out, same as foxes.

OTTER are cased and stretched fur side in. The pelt being thick and heavy, takes several days to dry properly. They are shipped flesh side out. Sea otter are handled the same as fox, lynx and marten, that is, fur side out.

BEAVER are split but stretched round and should be left in the hoop or stretcher for several days.

BEAR should be handled open and stretched carefully. In skinning be careful and leave nose, claws and ears on the hide.

WOLVES can be handled same as bear, also wolverine.

FISHER should be cased and stretched flesh side out, but may be sent to market same as foxes or fur out.

MARTEN should be stretched and dried on boards, fur side in, but turned as soon as dried.

OPOSSUM are stretched on boards fur side in and are left in that condition after removing the boards. Cut the tails off when skinning — they have no value.

116

MUSKRAT should be stretched fur side in and a few days on the boards is sufficient. They are left as taken off, that is, fur side in. Cut the tails off when skinning — they are worthless.

WEASEL should be cased, fur side in. The pelts are thin and soon dry. Leave fur side in after taking off boards.

BADGER are split and should be nailed to the inside of a building to dry.

CIVET CAT should be cased and stretched on boards fur side in. When dry remove boards and leave fur side in.

RING TAIL CATS should be cased and after removing boards are generally left fur side in for market.

WILD CAT are cased and stretched on boards. They may be turned fur out or left as taken from the stretchers, fur side in.

HOUSE CAT are cased and stretched on boards fur side in. They are sent to market usually fur side in.

RABBITS are cased fur in and, as the pelt is thin, soon dry. They are shipped fur side in.

PANTHER are treated much the same as bear. Care should be taken in skinning to leave claws, ears, nose, etc., on the skin for mounting purposes.

My experience has been that the house which makes only four grades of prime goods is the house that you will receive the largest checks from for your collection, writes a Michigan collector of 50 years' experience. So many grades quoted makes it possible for a firm to successfully squelch you a little every time you ship and yet you can have no reasonable excuse to complain for when you ship, you know that in some houses there is a grade for nearly every skin you send. So I, for one, would rather risk the fewer grades.

A trapper from Wisconsin says: For sample, say mink are worth from 25 cents to $3.00. There would be 275 prices between the extremes. Now if he is a fur buyer I certainly pity the trappers that would have to take those 275 different prices for their mink. A man should be able to know the difference between grades No. 1, 2, 3 and 4, and when he does he is then able to give a fair and honest price for every skin he buys. If he doesn't know the difference then, he had better get a job clerking in a hotel or sawing wood.

117

Many have requested that the difference in the various grades of skins be explained and for their benefit, as well as others of little experience, the following may prove instructive.

Raw furs are assorted into four grades, viz: No. 1, No. 2, No. 3 and No. 4. With the exception of skunk and muskrat most houses subdivide the No. 1 skins into large, medium and small. In addition to this many firms quote a range of prices about as follows: Mink, Northern New York, large $6.00 to $8.00. Would it not be more satisfactory to quote one price only?

It is generally known that Minnesota mink are large. From that state a No. 1 medium mink is as large as a No. 1 large from Maine, where mink are rather small. But as the dealers on their price lists quote the various states and sections, why not quote one price only as follows:

MINK, NORTHERN NEW YORK, NO. 1

Large,	Medium,	Small,	No. 2,	No. 3,	No. 4,
$7.00.	$5.00.	$3.00	$1.50.	$0.75.	$0.20

These figures, of course, are only given for illustration and are not meant to show value.

Furs from the various parts of North America have their peculiar characteristics and it is easy for the man of experience to tell in what part of the country a pelt was caught. It may be shipped by a collector hundreds of miles from where caught, but if there are many in the collection the expert will soon detect it. This knowledge, however, only comes with years of experience.

Prime skins are those caught during cold weather and the pelt after drying a few days is bright and healthy appearing.

Unprime skins are those that turn blue or black after being stretched for a time. Usually the darker the pelt the poorer the fur. If only slightly blued the pelt may go back only one grade, while if black it is apt to be no better than No. 3 or No. 4 and may be trash of no value.

Springy skins, as the name indicates, are those taken toward the last of the season or in the spring and tho often prime pelted, have begun to shed. The beginner is often deceived, for he thinks if the pelt is prime, the fur is. Foxes and other animals are often "rubbed" toward spring, which of course lessens their value.

A No. 1 skin must be not only average in size but free from cuts, etc. No unprime skin will grade better than No. 2.

Skunk, to be No. 1 or black, must be prime in pelt, fair size and stripe not extending beyond the shoulders. The day that only "star black" were taken for No. 1 is passed, for most trappers and shippers know better now.

A No. 2, or short striped skunk, is prime and the stripes, if narrow, may extend nearly to the tail. A small No. 1 or a blued No. 1 is graded No. 2.

A No. 3 or long stripe has two stripes extending the entire length, but there must be as much black between the stripes as either of the white stripes.

In some of the states, such as Minnesota, Iowa, the Dakotas, etc., skunk are large and are nearly all striped the same — long narrow stripes — but owing to their size they are worth about the same as the eastern short stripe or No. 2.

A No. 4, broad or white skunk, is prime but has two broad stripes extending down the back. Most dealers class skunk as No. 4 if either white stripe contains more white than there is black between the two stripes.

All unprime skunk are graded down to No. 2, 3 and 4 according to depth of fur and stripe. A No. 1 skunk in stripe, but blue, becomes a No. 2, or if badly blued No. 3 or 4; a No. 2 skunk in stripe but blue becomes a No. 3; a No. 3 in stripe but blue, a No. 4; a No. 4 in stripe but blue generally goes into trash. In fact, if badly blued, any of the grades may be thrown to trash.

Muskrat are assorted into four grades — spring, winter, fall and kitts. Spring rats are known as No. 1; winter, No. 2; fall, No. 3; Kitts, No. 4.

No. 1 or spring rats are those taken in March and April. The pelt is then of a reddish color and is entirely free from dark spots. A few spring rats may be caught earlier than March, but so long as they show dark spots they are not No. 1.

No. 2, or winter rats, are pretty well furred, but there are dark streaks and spots in the hide usually on the back.

No. 3 or fall are not full furred and the pelt is far from prime. The dark streaks show much more than later in the season.

No. 4, or kitts, are only partly grown or if larger are badly damaged.

Opossum is the only animal that may have a "prime" pelt but an "unprime" coat of fur. This makes opossum rather difficult to assort unless turned fur side out.

If opossum have been properly skinned and stretched they will, when unprime, show a dark blue spot on the under side at the throat. The plainer this spot the poorer the fur.

Good unprime skins are No. 2; poor unprime skins, No. 3; the very poor and stagey, no fur, are No. 4, generally known as trash and of no value.

The other fur-bearers, such as mink, otter, beaver, fox, wolves, lynx, wild cat, fisher, raccoon, bear, badger, civet cat, weasel, etc., are graded much the same that is, all skins to be No. 1 must be caught in season, when the fur is prime, at which time the "pelt" is healthy appearing — never blue or black — must be of average size, correctly skinned, handled and free of cuts or shot holes.

Skins may be unprime from several causes, viz: caught too early, improperly handled, under size, etc. Unprime skins are graded No. 2, 3 and 4 according to how inferior they are. The fairly well furred unprime skins are graded No. 2; the low furred unprime skins are thrown to No. 3; the poorly furred are thrown to No. 4, while low stagey skins go to trash.

Some skins altho prime are so small that they grade No. 3. This, however, is the exception rather than the rule. Usually if prime, the under size will only put the skin down one grade.

I have bought some for a number of years, writes a collector, and know that some trappers are like some farmers, they want as much money for a bushel of dirty wheat as their neighbor gets for a bushel of clean wheat. I have had skunk and opossum hides offered me that had a pound or two of tainted fat on them, and skins that were taken out of season, for which they expect to get No. 1 prices.

There are some who stretch their skins in the shape of an oblong triangle and leave flesh enough on to make their dinner. Stretch your hides as near the shape of the animal as possible; don't try to make a muskrat hide as long as a mink, or a mink as wide as a muskrat. Catch in season, flesh carefully, stretch in good shape, always take bone out of tails, keep in an airy building until dry and then you will not have to grumble so much at the buyer in regard to prices.

CHAPTER XXVII

FROM ANIMAL TO MARKET

Under this title, says an experienced Western trapper, I shall endeavor to show my brother trappers how to handle pelts:

As soon as I get in from my traps (I use a team and wagon), I feed team, dogs and self, then I proceed to skin the game in the usual manner; when game is all skinned I put on my fleshing suit, made of rubber cloth like that buggy curtains are made of, get out my fleshing boards, of which I have three sizes — large, medium and small — for each kind of cased skins except rat, which I flesh with thumb and knife. The fleshing boards are like Fig. 1 on enclosed diagram, made of 1 inch pine free from knots and dressed on both sides, 3 feet 6 inches long, and for skunk 3/4 in. and 10 in. wide, tapered up to a blunt point, edges rounded and sandpapered smooth. These boards can be made of other sizes so as to fit larger or smaller pelts of other kinds.

FIG. 1.

FLESHING BOARD

For a flesher I have tried nearly everything imaginable, dull knives, hardwood scrapers, etc., but have abandoned them all for the hatchet. I use an old lath hatchet head and use it tolerably sharp; I proceed as follows: Put pelt on board but do not fasten, grip lower edge with left hand, pull down hard, place point of board against breast and use hatchet with right, pushing down and holding hatchet nearly flat; use plenty of elbow grease; as fast as you get a strip cleaned off turn hide a little but do not flesh on edge of board. It may not work good at first and you may cut one or two hides, but you will soon get the knack.

Fig. 2.

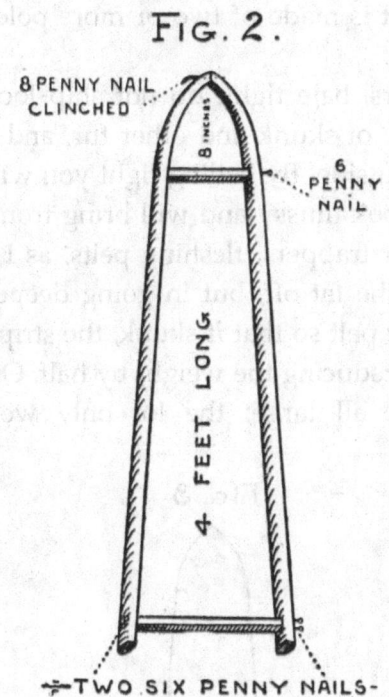

8 PENNY NAIL CLINCHED

6 PENNY NAIL

8 INCHES

4 FEET LONG

–?–TWO SIX PENNY NAILS–

STRETCHING FRAME

If possible take a bitch skunk for the first as they flesh easier, and be sure there are no burrs or chunks of mud in the fur, or you will cut a hole the size of the burr. Now for the stretchers. In Fig. 2 is what I use; it is something of my own invention, and there is no

123

patent on it. It is made of any wood that will split straight, and the dimensions are as follows: Pieces are 4 ft. long by 1 3/8 in. dressed smooth; pieces are 1 1/2 X 3/8 in.; will say for large skunks here they would be 10 in. and 4 1/2 in. To frame you must soak or steam the long pieces; mitre the ends and fasten with 3d finishing nails clinched. Then place in position 1 in. from ends and fasten with two 6d finishing nails; place in position and pull up to 8 in. from nose and fasten: now chamfer off edges and sandpaper smooth.

I like this stretcher, as it airs both sides of pelt and will dry them in half the time. Fig 3 shows manner of fastening pelt; on belly side it can be drawn down and fastened to tail pieces with sack needle and twine; it is made of two or more poles fastened in the shape of a hoop.

In shipping furs, bale tight; do not ship loose in sack; place mink and rat inside of skunk and other fur, and always place the toughest pelts on outside. By bailing tight you will avoid crinkling and they will not look mussy and will bring from 5 to 10 per cent more. Now, brother trappers, fleshing pelts, as I understand it, is not merely taking the fat off, but in going deeper and taking the flesh clean from the pelt so that if skunk, the stripe will show clear the full length and reducing the weight by half. On February 2nd. I shipped 15 skunk, all large; the lot only weighed 9 pounds including sack.

FIG. 3

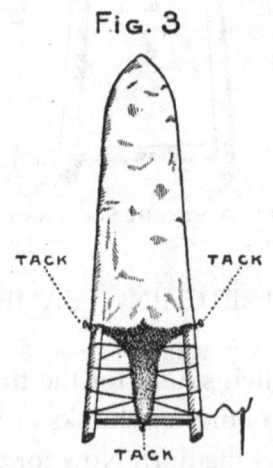

SKIN ON STRETCHER

When stretching skunk and otter skins, if the weather is warm, split the tails, open and tack flat. Split open half way all others that have fur tails. Open pelts can be stretched in hoops made of one or more poles an inch or so in diameter, and sewed in with a sack needle and heavy twine.

In stretching do not get the pelt so wide that the fur looks thin, or so long and narrow that it looks as if a horse had been hitched to each end. Keep the natural shape of the animal as much as possible, dry in a cool, airy place inside, or on the north side of a building and away from fire.

Baling — here is where the expert trapper shows his craft, and in baling you will see him wipe off all surplus fat and dirt and place the heavy pelts on the outside of his pack. The lighter furs, such as mink, marten, cat, etc., will be placed inside of the skins that are heavier. For instance: From four to eight rats or mink, inside of a fox or skunk. He will place the head of one to the tail of another, the tails folded in. He now ties a cord tightly around each end, placing them on a square of burlap, and with sack needle and twine draws up the sides as tight as he can; then he folds in the ends and sews up snug. Furs thus packed reach the market in good shape, and not such as they would if crammed promiscuously into a sack.

Fig. 4.

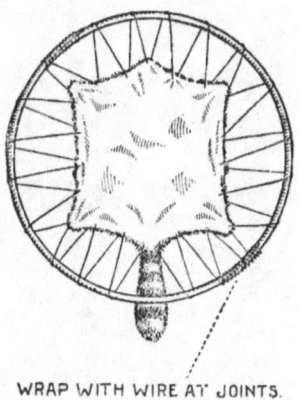

WRAP WITH WIRE AT JOINTS.

WRAP WITH WIRE AT JOINTS

In conclusion, boys, let me suggest a maxim or two for your guidance: "Prime caught and well handled furs always bring top prices." "Take pride in your catch, no matter how small."

While the heading of this chapter is "From Animal to Market" it is well when shipping to request the dealer to grade and send value. If satisfactory, write to send on check. If not satisfactory, have dealer return furs.

When shipping furs under these conditions see that no green skins are sent — only properly cured ones.

While some dealers offer to pay expressage both ways we hardly think this fair and if no deal is made the dealer should pay the expressage one way and the shipper the other.

The Hunter-Trader-Trapper, published at Columbus, Ohio, in the interests of hunters, trappers and dealers in raw furs contains a great deal of information that will be of value along the line of shipping furs as well as trapping methods, etc.

CHAPTER XXVIII

STEEL TRAPS

This book would not be complete without at least a few pages devoted to steel traps. While a few steel traps were in use prior to 1850, yet it has only been since that date that they have come into general use. During recent years they have become cheaper and trappers in all parts of America are using them in greater numbers.

Professional trappers in the North, Northwest and Southwest often have out lines many miles long and use 200 to 350 steel traps of the various sizes.

Each of the three main sets — land, water and snow are used in various ways and to describe all of these would require a book.

Steel traps are made in various sizes from No. 0 to No. 6, to meet the requirements of trappers for the various animals. The best traps manufactured are the Newhouse made by the well-known trap manufacturers — Oneida Community, Ltd., Oneida, N. Y. A brief description of these follows:

Spread of Jaws, 3 1/2 inches. This, the smallest trap made, is used mostly for catching the gopher, a little animal which is very troublesome to western farmers, and also rats and other vermin. It has a sharp grip and will hold larger game, but should not be overtaxed.

Spread of Jaws, 4 inches. This Trap is used for catching muskrats and other small animals, and sold in greater numbers than any other size. Its use is well understood by professional trappers and it is the most serviceable size for catching skunks, weasels, rats and such other animals as visit poultry houses and barns.

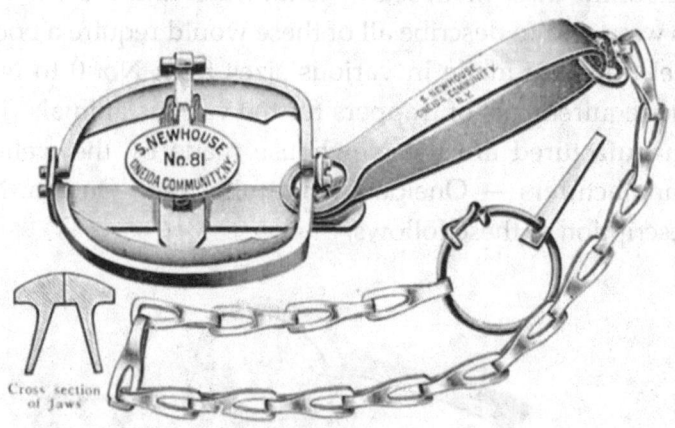

Spread of Jaws, 4 inches. Occasionally animals free themselves from traps by gnawing their legs off just below the trap jaws, where the flesh is numb from pressure. Various forms of traps have been experimented with to obviate this difficulty. The Webbed Jaws shown above have proved very successful in this respect.

Noting the cross-section of the jaws, as illustrated at the left, it is plain the animal can only gnaw off its leg at a point quite a distance below the meeting edges. The flesh above the point of amputation and below the jaws will swell and make it impossible to pull the leg stump out of the trap.

The No. 81 Trap corresponds in size with the regular No. 1 Newhouse.

Spread of Jaws — 91, 5 1/4 inches; 91 1/2, 6 1/4 inches. The double jaws take an easy and firm grip so high up on the muskrat that he can not twist out. A skunk cannot gnaw out either.

These traps are especially good for muskrat, mink, skunk and raccoon.

All parts of the No. 91 except the jaws are the same size as the regular No. 1 Newhouse, while the 91 1/2 corresponds to the regular No. 1 1/2.

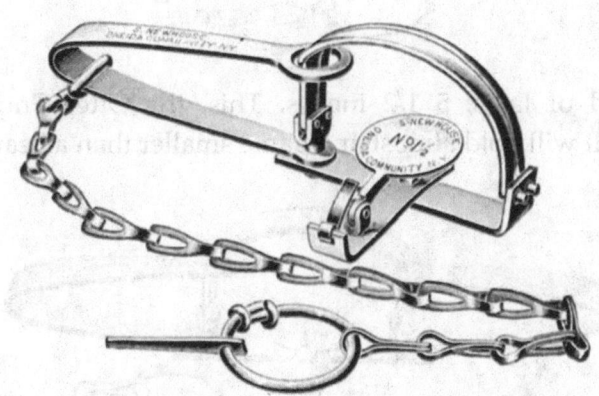

Spread of Jaws, 4 7/8 inches. This size is called the Mink Trap. It is, however, suitable for catching the woodchuck, skunk, etc.

Professional trappers often use it for catching foxes. It is very convenient in form and is strong and reliable.

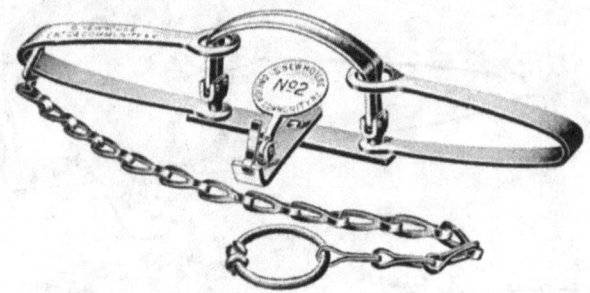

Spread of Jaws, 4 7/8 inches. The No. 2 Trap is called the Fox Trap. Its spread of jaws is the same as the No. 1 1/2 but having two springs it is, of course, much stronger.

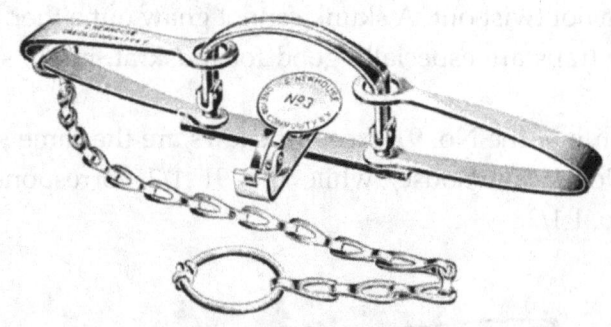

Spread of Jaws, 5 1/2 inches. This, the Otter Trap, is very powerful. It will hold almost any game smaller than a bear.

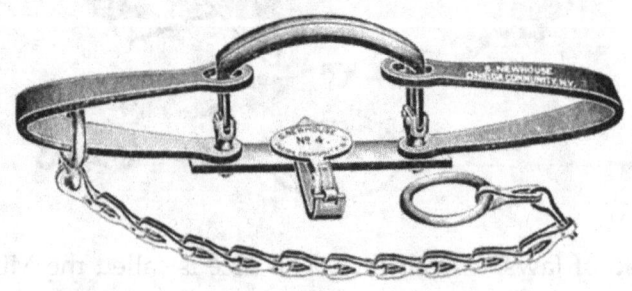

Spread of Jaws, 6 1/2 inches. This is the regular form of Beaver Trap. It is longer than the No. 3 Trap, and has one inch greater spread of jaws. It is a favorite with those who trap and hunt for a living in the Northwest and Canada. It is also extensively used for trapping the smaller wolves and coyotes in the western stock raising regions.

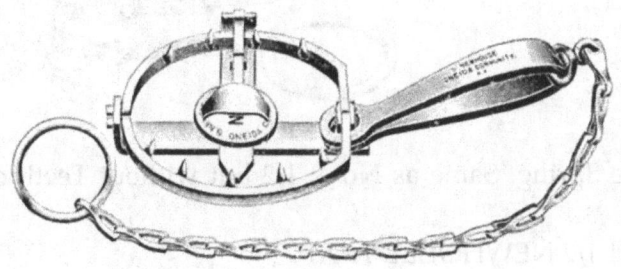

Spread of Jaws, 6 1/2 inches. In some localities the otter grows to an unusual size, with great proportionate strength, so that the manufacturers have been led to produce an especially large and strong pattern. All the parts are heavier than the No. 2 1/2, the spread of jaws greater and the spring stiffer.

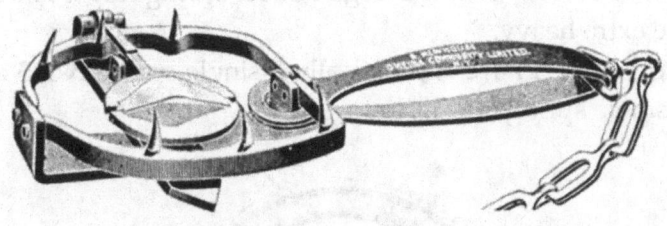

Spread of Jaws, 5 inches. The above cut represents a Single Spring Otter Trap. It is used more especially for catching otter on their "slides." For this purpose a thin, raised plate of steel is adjusted to the pan so that when the trap is set the plate will be a trifle higher than the teeth on the jaws. The spring is very powerful, being the same as used on the No. 4 Newhouse Trap. The raised plate can be readily detached if desired, making the trap one of general utility.

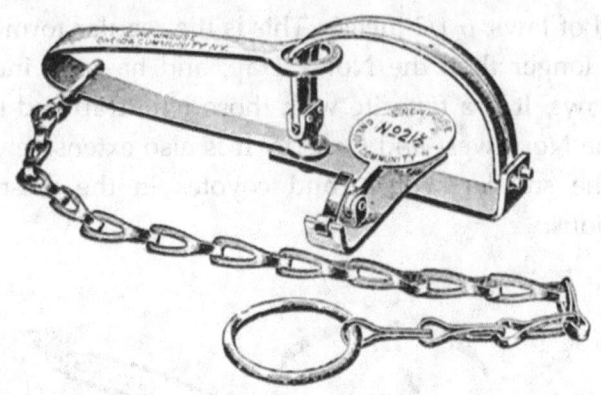

Single Spring. Same as No. 2 1/2 but without Teeth or Raised Plate.

No. 31 1/2 NEWHOUSE TRAP.

Single Spring. Same as No. 3 1/2 but without Teeth or Raised Plate.

Spread of Jaws — No. 21 1/2, 5 1/4 inches; No. 31 1/2, 6 1/2 inches. These Traps are the largest smooth jaw, single spring sizes that are made. Professional trappers will find these especially valuable when on a long trapping line, as they are more compact and easier to secrete than the large double spring traps. The springs are made extra heavy.

Note. — The 21 1/2 is practically a single spring No. 3 and the 31 1/2 a single spring No. 4.

Spread of Jaws, 6 1/2 inches. This Trap is the same in size as the No. 4 Beaver, but has heavier and stiffer springs and offset jaws, which allow the springs to raise higher when the animal's leg is in the trap, and is furnished with teeth sufficiently close to prevent the animal from pulling its foot out.

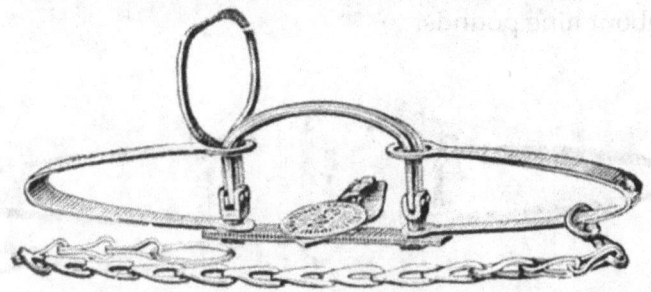

Clutch Detachable — Trap can be used with or without it.

Spread of Jaws, No. 23, 5 1/2 inches; No. 24, 6 1/4 inches. The inventor of this attachment claims to have had wonderful success with it in taking beaver. The trap should be set with the clutch end farthest from shore. The beaver swims with his fore legs folded back against his body, and when he feels his breast touch the bank he puts them down. The position of the trap can be so calculated that he will put his fore legs in the trap, when the clutch will seize him across the body and hold him securely.

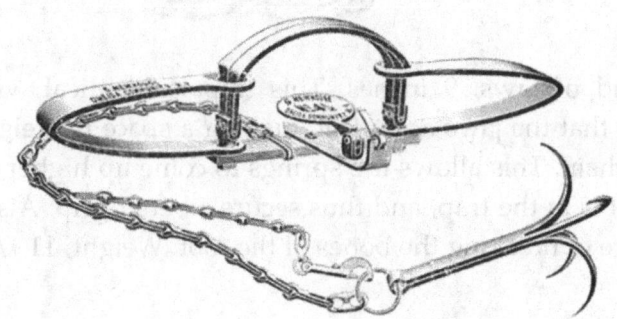

In response to a demand for a new model of the Newhouse Trap especially adapted to catching wolves, the manufacturers have perfected a trap which is numbered 4 1/2 and is called the "Newhouse Wolf Trap."

133

This trap has eight inches spread of jaw, with other parts in proportion, and is provided with a pronged "drag," a heavy snap and an extra heavy steel swivel and chain, five feet long, warranted to hold 2,000 pounds. The trap complete with chain and "drag" weighs about nine pounds.

Spread of Jaws, 9 inches. This trap is intended for catching small sized bears. In design it is exactly like the standard No. 5 Bear Trap, only that the parts are all somewhat smaller. Weight, 11 1/4 pounds each.

Spread of Jaws, 9 inches. This trap is identical with No. 5 excepting that the jaws are offset, making a space five-eighths inch between them. This allows the springs to come up higher when the bear's foot is in the trap, and thus secure a better grip. Also there is less chance of breaking the bones of the foot. Weight, 11 1/4 pounds each.

Spread of Jaws, 11 3/4 inches. This trap weighs nineteen pounds. It is used for taking the common black bear and is furnished with a very strong chain.

Spread of Jaws, 11 3/4 inches. To meet the views of certain hunters whose judgment is respected, the manufacturers designed a style of jaw for the No. 5 trap, making an offset of 3/4 of an inch, so as to allow the springs to come up higher when the bear's leg is in the trap. This gives the spring a better grip. Those wishing this style should specify "No. 15."

Spread of Jaws, 16 inches. Weight, complete, 42 pounds. This is the strongest trap made. We have never heard of anything getting out of it when once caught. It is used to catch lions and tigers, as well as the great Grizzly Bears of the Rocky Mountains.

This cut illustrates Bear Chain Clevis and Bolt, intended as a substitute for the ring on the end of the trap chain, when desired.

With this clevis a loop can be made around any small log or tree without the trouble of cutting to fit the ring. The chain is made five feet long, suitable for any clog, and the prices of bear traps fitted with it are the same as with the regular short chain and ring.

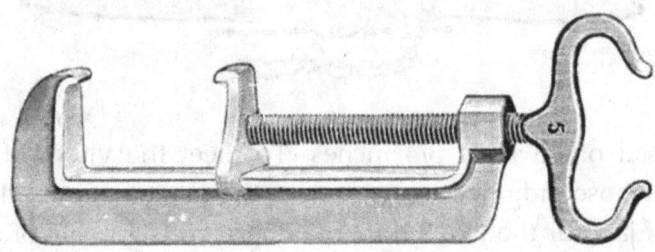

Every trapper knows how difficult it is to set a large trap alone in the woods, especially in cold weather, when the fingers are stiff, and the difficulty is greatly increased when one has to work in a boat. One of these clamps applied to each spring will by a few turns of the thumb-screws, bend the springs to their places, so that the pan may be adjusted without difficulty. No. 4 Clamp can be used on any trap smaller than No. 4 1 /2. No. 5 and 6 are strong clamps, carefully made and especially adapted to setting the large traps Nos. 4 1/2 to 6. They dispense with the inconvenient and dangerous use of levers. With them one can easily set these powerful traps. These clamps are also useful about camp for other purposes.

END OF DEADFALLS AND SNARES

www.ingramcontent.com/pod-product-compliance
Lightning Source LLC
Chambersburg PA
CBHW011507170626
46812CB00008B/3002